"There's humor, conflict and a strong empathy with 13-year-old Sheila, who casts off boredom and loneliness to join in the life of the school. Miss Richardson tells her story in the idiom of youth which should appeal to all readers."—Rochester *Democrat & Chronicle*

"The characters are always real and the teachers are people, too. The conversation is very contemporary. The atmosphere and characters are strong." (Starred Review) —*Kirkus Reviews*

"This is an exciting story about young people who are as modern as tomorrow, but as natural as yesterday. The way they handle freedom of choice, with indirect guidance from their teachers, makes for a story that is different as well as entertaining."—Shreveport *Journal*

Apples Every Day

by Grace Richardson

A HARPER TROPHY BOOK
HARPER & ROW, PUBLISHERS
New York, Evanston, San Francisco, London

Standard Book Number: 06–440045–X

First published in 1965. 3rd printing, 1966.
First Harper Trophy Book printing, 1973.

For Antony Burpee

Apples Every Day

*R*ain poured down upon the city of Montreal. Water dripped from raincoats and umbrellas, making puddles on the smooth gray floor inside Central Station. The hands of the big clock stood at ten to six. It was September, the day after Labor Day, the day children give up their summer's freedom to return to school.

The carriage in which Sheila Davis sat was almost full. She sat tensely on the seat facing Mother and Stan, wondering how many more bright, encouraging remarks she could bear.

"Really, dear, boarding school can be *fun*," Mother was saying. "Pillow fights in the dorm, you know, and midnight feasts, and secret societies, and—oh, things like that. . . ." Her voice trailed away. She looked at her daughter with an anxious little frown.

"And leftover stew," Stan put in dryly. Stan was Sheila's new stepfather.

"Oh, I'm sure the food will be good at Kenner," Mother exclaimed. "After all, it *is* a progressive school—they'll probably fatten you up on wheat germ and tiger's milk. And think of the freedom, dear, compared to most schools, especially boarding schools—no exams, no ugly uniform, and so on."

"I'd *like* to wear a uniform," Sheila muttered sulkily.

"Now, dear, you're just being contrary." Mother frowned

anxiously again. "You do realize you don't have to stay if you aren't happy, dear? We just want you to give Kenner a chance. You may like it much better than your old day school; it's a special school, and you've always been rather a special child."

"Special" means "neurotic," Sheila thought bitterly; so I'm being sent off to a nuthouse where I belong. And so Stan won't have to be bothered with a child who isn't his and just gets in the way.

"Well," Stan said uneasily, "I guess we'd better get going now, Sheila. Got everything you need?"

"Oh, but we've still a few minutes," Mother protested.

Stan shifted from one foot to another. "I always find long farewells more painful than a short, clean break."

"All right, then." Mother bent down and kissed Sheila on the cheek. "You *will* try and be happy, darling, won't you?" she pleaded. "You know how much we want you to be happy."

"Yes, Mother."

Sheila sat quietly, waiting for them to leave. Stan took Mother's arm and led her away, though she hung back, smiling anxiously and waving. . . . At last they were gone. It was a relief not to have to talk with them anymore, but she was a bit resentful. She looked at her new watch: five more minutes. Couldn't they have waited just five minutes? Daddy had sent her the watch as a going-away-to-school present, but he hadn't come to see her off at all. *He* didn't care, either . . . but she knew she was being unfair. Daddy couldn't very well come all the way from Vancouver just to see her off to school.

Suddenly she was full of hate. She didn't want to hate Mother or Stan right now, that would be too much to bear; but she must hate somebody. Somebody unimportant but hateful. . . . Yes, Miss Simmons, the math teacher at her former school, with her wispy gray hair and crisp, humorless voice. Sheila sat and hated her fiercely. Then she opened the movie magazine Stan had

2

bought her to read on the train. The beautiful faces looked out at her from their world of glamor. She almost forgot Kenner School.

Jerry Dressler boarded the train alone. The carriage was crowded, but he found one empty seat and slipped in beside the window. He opened the paperback mystery begun on the plane to Montreal, then put it aside; he didn't really feel like reading right now. It was more interesting to look around at his fellow passengers, wondering which of the younger ones might be bound for Kenner School like himself. A quartet of black-uniformed girls talking in French didn't seem too likely. But the two boys across the aisle, both about his own age, might very well be schoolmates of his.

They sat energetically chewing gum while they read magazines. The one browsing through *Playboy* had long, shaggy dark hair. He wore three very ancient sweaters in shades of faded blue, all full of holes, so that bits of all three showed at once. At his side, leaning against his arm, was a battered banjo case. The other boy, who wore a natty gray tweed suit, had smooth blond hair and narrow green eyes in a pale face. He looked no more than fourteen at the most; but on his upper lip was a neat blond mustache. He was reading *MacLean's*.

"Hey, Mike, Pierre—hi!" another boy yelled from the opposite end of the carriage. "Have a good summer?"

They looked up briefly. "Hi! Oh, sure."

"I had a great time myself, but still, it's good to be going back. Say, Mike, where's the python?"

(*Python?* Jerry listened with interest.)

"In a zoo or somewhere," the dark boy replied, shifting an enormous wad of gum to one cheek. "It started getting too affectionate with Mum, so she gave it away—I was furious."

"Aw, gee!"

"I wanted to get a boa to bring this year, but they cost five dollars a foot, and I'm broke. So I brought my banjo instead."

"Gee, it won't be the same without your python. He was the best pet we've ever had."

Yes, Jerry decided, they must be Kenner students. He was relieved to know that he would not have to share dormitory life with a boa constrictor. The dark boy called Mike continued to read; but all through the carriage Jerry heard other greetings exchanged, girls' and boys' voices, all apparently delighted to be returning to school. Nobody else seemed new like Jerry himself.

He sighed deeply, but not because he felt lonely. He usually made friends easily. If the two boys across the aisle hadn't been so absorbed in their magazines, he would have struck up a conversation with them right now. It was just the whole pointless business of coming to Kenner School in the first place. Oh, well; he had heard some rumor about the school being bankrupt and liable to close any day. So maybe he wouldn't have to stay too long.

He opened his mystery novel. . . . *"Mr. Allen," she exclaimed tremulously, her jet-black eyes deep pools of fear, "you must believe me. My husband is trying to murder me. . . ."*

Only sixteen, still in high school, Sue Anne Miller is already a successful model. Soon to make her acting debut, she will appear on Playhouse 60 *in December. Moviegoer salutes a bright young talent. . . .* Sheila eyed the girl's pretty face and shining blond hair with envy. Only three years and a bit older than herself . . .

The loudspeaker announced, blurrily bilingual: *"Le train pour,* the train for Bridge Street, St. Lambert, St. Hubert, Mont Bruno, St. Basil le Grand, Beloeil, Otterburn Park, St. Hilaire, St. Hilaire East, and St. Hyacinthe, *départ sur la voie numéro dix-sept,* now leaving on Track Seventeen. *En voiture!* All aboard!"

Sheila stared as two breathless, heavily laden girls burst into the carriage. A tap on the window, a pretty woman's smiling face, waves from the girls . . . then a jerk, a heave, a groan, and the train began to move. Both girls collapsed upon the seat facing Sheila's.

"Well, we made it, anyway," gasped one of them. "Gee, Mummy's so graceful and chic, it just makes me *sick*." The girl was very tall, slim, and awkward, perhaps thirteen years old, dressed in a loose smocklike dress of red and black stripes and high-heeled red shoes. She looked like an overladen pack horse, hung about with shoulder-strap bags, a camera, dirty white sneakers, dirty white skates, two shopping bags, a tennis racket, and a guitar. Her untidy red hair dripped around a pink, rather pimply face dotted with dabs of Clearasil.

The other girl was small, graceful, and very pretty. Her blond hair fell to her shoulders, straight and shining; she had a delicate nose and bright sapphire-blue eyes. She wore a loose pink jersey and tight pink slacks. On her lap she held a small plaid suitcase protectively, with both arms, as though it were a baby. Eying both girls cautiously over her magazine, Sheila noticed at one end of the case a large hole covered with wire mesh but couldn't see what was inside. She hoped fervently it wasn't a cat.

The tall girl jumped up again and waved wildly. "Mike, Pierre—hi! Oh, *Mike,* you brought your *banjo*—great! We can have a hootenanny sometime! Hey, *Pierre*"—her voice rose to a squeak; her eyes, red-brown like her hair, widened—"you've grown a mus*tache!*"

Turning her head, Sheila saw a blond boy a few seats back smile and finger his upper lip. "It's a fake," he confessed,

5

without embarrassment. He had a slight French accent. "I was curious to see how I'd look with one."

"Gee, it looks *fabulous!* Don't *ever* take it off. Say, Mike, I've got a guitar!"

"Great," mumbled the dark boy through his chewing gum, still absorbed in *Playboy*.

"I only know one song," the tall girl went on eagerly. "I just got the guitar yesterday. My fingers are killing me."

She began unloading herself of purses, skates, bags—heaping them around her and on the floor. The small blond girl bent over the wire-mesh window in the suitcase and crooned, "Is oo comfy, wittle baby? Ahh, he's sleeping soundly. Those tranquilizers did the trick." Watching uneasily, Sheila prayed, Oh, please, let it not be a cat!

"Say, Sally, did you know?" The tall girl was tuning her guitar. "We're going to have just one roommate this year—somebody new."

"Just one? But there are usually four in that room."

"Yes, but there are only three new kids in the whole school this year."

"Only *three?* Last year there were seven!"

"Well, it seems the school isn't as popular as it used to be. Mum says people are losing confidence in its future because the Kenners are in debt and the school might have to close down next year or sometime. Isn't it sad? Anyway, I hope our new roommate won't be a drip." She made a few experimental, slightly dissonant strums. "Well, I guess that'll do." She leaned back, strummed, and sang in a thin treble:

> Love, O love, O careless love,
> Love, O love, O careless love,
> Love, O love, O careless love, O
> Love, O love, O careless love.

"That's the only verse I know so far—"

Sheila sneezed suddenly, and both girls looked up as though noticing her for the first time.

They saw a rather sallow face, with sharp cheekbones and a long thin mouth. Her hair was a dull brown, dry at the ends, greasy at the scalp. She met their curious gaze sullenly, looking back with large, shiny dark brown eyes.

"Want a Kleenex?" asked the tall girl kindly, producing a wrinkled, crumb-spattered one from her pocket. "Or an aspirin?"

"No, thanks." Sheila's voice was faint and hoarse. The worst had happened: there was a cat in that suitcase. But she couldn't bring herself to complain to these cheerful, self-assured girls.

"Say!" the tall one exclaimed. "Are you going to Kenner too?"

"Yes."

"Great! Maybe you're our new roommate." She eyed her with a faint frown. "Well—you don't *look* drippy. We don't mind if you're neurotic, just so long as you aren't a drip. Anyway, I'm Mimi Holly, and this is Sally Green."

"Hi," said the blond girl pleasantly.

"I'm Sheila Da—" Sheila's nose tickled, and her last name turned into a sneeze.

"Gee, you *do* have a cold," Mimi exclaimed sympathetically. "Here, let me give you something." She began rummaging in one of her purses, which seemed to be stuffed with small bottles.

"It's not a cold," Sheila confessed hoarsely. Her eyes were growing watery. "It's—well, I guess there must be a cat in that plaid suitcase. I'm allergic to cats."

Sally glared at her as though personally insulted.

"You mean—you're allergic to my darling baby boy even through his *case?*"

7

"I can't help it," said Sheila miserably. "I like cats, but I have this allergy when I get near them."

"Then you probably don't *really* like them at all, subconsciously. Rosalie Dennis—she's one of our teachers—"

"She's *fabulous*," Mimi gushed.

"Mimi adores her, but I don't, she's too . . . Well, you'll find out. But she *is* smart, and she says all allergies are—are—"

"Psychotic?" Mimi suggested uncertainly.

"No, I don't think so. No, *psychosomatic*." Sally brought out the word triumphantly. "All allergies are just psychosomatic."

"I have twenty-two allergies," said Mimi proudly, and began ticking them off on her fingers. "Wool, fish, nuts, celery, pollen, hay, dust, chocolate, horses . . . oh, lots more; I never can keep track of them all. I have a list somewhere. But luckily not cats—since I'm going to room with one." She looked at Sheila in sympathetic concern. "Gee, if you *are* our new roommate, you're going to have a pretty miserable year."

Sheila was feeling very sorry for herself. She was close to tears now, but her eyes were so teary already from close proximity to the cat, nobody would notice if she started to cry. Nobody would realize she was unhappy as well as allergic. "I didn't know you could bring pets to school," she muttered.

"Oh, sure," said Mimi. "I had a goldfish, but it went down the drain. And Mike—he's the boy with the banjo—he had a fabulous python, four feet long. He used to wear it to class."

"It only ate once a week," Sally put in, her bright blue eyes narrowing with pleasure at the memory. "A mouse or a hamster. Everyone used to go and watch. The python would swallow them whole! It was great."

Mimi shuddered. "But awful for the poor mouse—I just couldn't *bear* it. I never *can* bear to see a poor helpless animal in pain, especially mice. I suffer *with* them. I go through *agony!* Maybe it sounds silly, but it's just the way I am."

"Even so," Sally insisted, "you never missed a single feeding."

Mimi pulled a fat book out of a shopping bag: *Anna Karenina*. "Okay, now, you two, shut up. I'm going to read. I've been trying to get through this all summer to impress Rosalie." She opened the book somewhere near the beginning, hunched over it, and frowned deeply.

The ancient railway bridge rumbled beneath them as the train crossed the wide St. Lawrence. Jerry looked out the window, through the rain, upon an expanse of gray-green water. They drew into St. Lambert at the other side of the bridge, then moved out into the rain-drenched countryside. How flat it was! Field after field, only an occasional tree to break the monotony. After the New York State he knew, he could really feel that he was in another country. It *felt* like Canada, it felt bigger and newer than the United States; but it also felt so empty, almost bleak. He had heard that people in the Province of Quebec were keen skiers; but where were the hills? The train stopped frequently at small villages: a group of nondescript houses, a couple of dilapidated barns, an enormous church, its spire gleaming with bright aluminum paint, and occasionally a big sign: BUVEZ COCA-COLA. "Only twenty miles from Montreal to St. Hilaire," Dad had said, but the train would take nearly an hour. Nearly an hour! It seemed interminable.

Jerry turned to see a rather sullen-looking girl in a dark green coat, about a year younger than himself (Jerry was fourteen), slip into the empty seat beside him. She was blowing her nose with a crumpled gray Kleenex; she looked as though she had been crying. Impulsively he asked, "Are you going to Kenner School?"

"Yes . . . I'm new this year."

"So'm I. In fact, we seem to be the only new ones on the train."

He looked at her sallow face, her unhappy dark eyes. One of

those kids who couldn't bear to leave the family nest, who would cry herself to sleep every night. And he could tell at one glance that, even if she got used to boarding school, she was not the type ever to be popular. Definitely not a person he'd want to be too friendly with, especially at the beginning, when he himself was new and it was so important to start off right. To discourage further conversation, he went back to his book. But he always preferred to have people like him, even if they weren't anybody he'd care to know well, so he added, "I guess we're due at St. Hilaire a little before seven," and gave her his most winning smile.

She smiled back, rather shyly, then glanced out the window beside him. "Look! That must be Mont St. Hilaire."

Jerry peered through the rain. The fields now flashing past were dotted with small frame houses, perched upon the flat ground like buildings on a Monopoly board. The countryside was beginning to look like one vast suburb. But in the distance Jerry could make out the dim shape of a mountain.

"Oh, good!" he exclaimed, cheering a little. "I guess we'll be able to ski this winter." He began to feel resigned to the coming year.

Chapter Two

Mr. Kenner met the train at St. Hilaire. He stood on the platform of the small country station, waving cheerily: a short, stout man with thick glasses which magnified his round brown eyes. Sheila and Jerry hung back, feeling very strange and new, as the others clustered around him, crying, "Hello, Willy!" He smiled at them and led the way to a dilapidated old green bus. Sheila, swept into the crowd, found herself seated beside Mimi.

"Mrs. Kenner's name is Bianca," Mimi told her as the others fought for seats. Sheila saw Jerry near the front. "But she prefers to be called 'Kenny'—isn't it a waste? Imagine having a romantic Italian name like that and not wanting *everyone* to use it!"

Sheila glanced uneasily over her shoulder. Sally and the cat case were seated several rows back, beside a freckle-faced boy. Oh, well, that was probably a safe distance. She didn't want to meet Mrs. Kenner with red eyes and a runny nose.

"Okay, kids," Willy called from the driver's seat. "Mimi, will you please put your things in the luggage rack, *not* on the floor. Mike, open the window for Gaby in case she's carsick. Well, everybody here? There ought to be thirty-three of you." He felt in all his pockets. He wore baggy corduroy trousers, an open-necked shirt, and an old tweed jacket. "Oh dear, I've lost the list. Well, which of you are the new ones? There should be three: Jerry Dressler— Hi, Jerry! I'm an old pal of your dad's! Um—Sheila Davis, Phillip Bruce."

After a good deal of arguing, everybody decided that Phillip Bruce was not present and had probably not been on the train. Willy shrugged his plump shoulders.

"Well, we'd better get going. Dinner will be waiting, and I'm sure you're all hungry."

The old bus backfired loudly, then lurched onto the road, away from the station; the mountain loomed behind, green and yellow in the early autumn. Sheila, who was feeling a bit better, suddenly realized she was very hungry. "What's the food like?" she asked Mimi. "Do you have kind of funny things—like tiger's milk?"

"*Tiger's* milk? Heavens, no! We have things like leftover stew. And lots of apples. What d'you expect at boarding school? I hope tonight is blancmange night. It's kind of revolting, but they put a blob of jam on top, and we stir and stir and see whose turns out the evenest pink." Sheila, saying nothing, couldn't help feeling Mimi looked well past the playing-with-food age.

The sky was darkening. The wet road shone in the headlights of the bus, but the rain had stopped. They drove through a village and out into flat, more open country. To their left flowed a broad stretch of river, the Richelieu.

Suddenly their view of the water was cut off by a tall un-clipped hedge. The bus slowed down and turned into a circular driveway. They saw a wide, wet lawn, overgrown with weeds and wild grass. "The place goes to pot during the holidays," Mimi said. "During the term we kids are supposed to take turns mowing the lawn. Of course they can't *make* us, and it's a dreadful job, so sometimes it *stays* a mess."

The bus lurched to a stop before a large, dirty red-brick Victorian house. The wide front steps gleamed with fresh green paint, which ended abruptly at the scarred, peeling door.

Jerry's heart sank. He had somehow expected a bright modern building, all metal and glass and weird architecture. This decayed dump suggested an ancient English boarding school, not a progressive Canadian one. But Sheila, who had also expected something clean and modern, was rather pleased. This made her think of the orphanage in *Jane Eyre,* one of the books she loved most.

"We'll have to go round by the kitchen door," Willy instructed them, "as the paint is still wet—Mike, stop!" But it was too late; Mike had already started up the steps. Meekly he came down again and followed the others around to the side of the house, leaving a trail of green footprints on the gravel.

Willy opened a door, and the thirty-two students crowded after him into a large, hot, very messy kitchen with greasy walls. A fat gray-haired woman was stirring something unappetizing-looking in a huge caldron. *"Bonjour, Madame!"* the children greeted her. She smiled and wiped her sweating face with a food-stained apron. *"Bonjour, mes enfants!* You enjoy your 'oliday, *hein?* Dinner, it is ready in the dining room."

"We'll eat now, then, while the soup's hot," said Willy, sampling the contents of the caldron thoughtfully. "Mnnn—not bad, Madame, not bad. But a bit bland." He picked up a small bottle. "Some oregano, I think"—and he sprinkled it very generously into the pot while Madame glowered and Mimi winced. "Oregano's one of my allergies," she muttered to Sheila.

"I'll carry this in for you," Willy told Madame, heaving the caldron off the stove and spilling a little on the floor. "Kids, just put your things down anywhere for the moment. You can go to your rooms when you've eaten."

After the dark shabbiness of the house's exterior and the squalor of the kitchen, the dining room was startling: an almost blinding glare of bright color. True, the tables and benches might have come straight from *Jane Eyre* or *Oliver Twist*, Sheila felt; but the long, high walls were covered, from ceiling to floor, with hundreds of pictures, many overlapping, some cut out of magazines and pasted together, others done in bright poster paint. There were outsize Coca-Cola bottles; advertising slogans in French and English; figures from well-known comic strips, with and without dialogue balloons; and a series of large neonlike signs in luminescent paint.

"Gee!" Sheila exclaimed. "What *wild* murals!"

"It's our Pop Art exhibit," said Mimi proudly. "Willy thought it'd be more fun, and cheaper, for us to decorate the walls than repaint. Everybody did them, the teachers too."

"The luminous paint work is mine," added the blond boy called Pierre, the boy with the mustache whom Sheila had seen on the train. "Rather effective, don't you think?"

"Not bad," said Jerry, coming up to inspect them.

"*I* did the Mary Worth cartoons," said Mimi. "Come on, let's eat!"

Dinner was buffet style. Everybody served himself from dishes on the sideboard: the caldron of soup, pots of baked beans, long loaves of French bread, jugs of milk and nonalcoholic cider, bowls of big, crisp red apples.

"What lovely apples!" said Sheila, who had been fearing blancmange.

"You won't think so when you've had apples morning, noon, and night all winter long," Mimi complained. "This is apple-orchard country, and apples are about the cheapest thing you can buy. We have baked apples, fried apples, stewed apples, apple pudding, apple pie, apple fritters, endless cider—and plain apples, of course, any time you want; the basement is stuffed with them. After a year in this place, you won't want to *look* at another apple." She pulled a large hunk off a loaf of bread and munched it gloomily. It was about the only thing present, besides apples, that she wasn't allergic to.

It was a restless meal, with a lot of talking, wandering from table to table, throwing food, and playing tricks with the salt cellar. "I get indigestion all the time here," Mimi told Sheila, leading her to a table. Most students were twelve to fifteen years old. Sheila noticed Jerry at the next table, talking to the shaggy-haired boy with the banjo—Mike, that was his name. Jerry looked cheerful and relaxed, as though already at home among all these strange kids. Surrounded by talk and laughter, Sheila felt a bit lost. There were so many of them! Well, no, not really; it was a very small school. They seemed many because they were all so strange. So many strange faces, so many strange names. How would she ever get to know them all?

While everyone was still eating, Sally, who was sitting at the same table as Jerry, let her cat out of his carrier to stretch his legs. Sheila had somehow expected a pedigreed Siamese, but instead she saw an enormous fat tabby with an ugly face and crossed eyes. She watched him anxiously, hoping he wouldn't come near her. Instead he jumped up on Sally's table. Several students clustered around, offering him scraps.

"Isn't he *adorable?*" gushed the girls. "Where did you *get* him, Sally? What's his name? He's the most divine cat I've ever *seen!*"

"He's called The Cat of Cats," said Sally, "because he's so adorably catlike." The boys were less enthusiastic; but when one pulled Cat's tail and earned a nasty scratch, they looked at Sally's pet with new respect. "He's very vicious," she said proudly. "Aren't oo, baby-puss?" She bent down to kiss his nose, but backed away as he lashed out with an enormous paw. "He's even vicious to me," she added just as proudly. "I keep his claws nice and long."

Suddenly Mrs. Kenner entered the room.

"Hello, Kenny!" several voices called. Everyone stopped playing with Sally's cat. There was something about Mrs. Kenner which attracted instant attention.

She was a slim, wiry little woman, darkly sun-tanned, with black eyes and coarse black hair piled high. She wore a bright green Paisley-print dress. Smiling around the room, she spoke in a deep, warm voice. "Hello, everybody! I hope you've all had as nice a holiday as Willy and I, but I also hope you old students are glad to be back. To tell the truth, much as we're glad to get rid of you every summer, after a while things get a bit dull without you."

Everyone smiled indulgently at her little joke. Somebody murmured, "She says that every year."

"It *is* good to be back, Kenny," Mimi exclaimed. "I told my family I'd miss them terribly, and I *meant* it at the time. But now I'm here, I don't miss them at all!" Everybody smiled again.

"Hello, Sheila." Kenny came across the room and shook Sheila's hand warmly. Sheila had met her before, at the interview in Montreal with her mother. Kenny had worn high heels then; now she wore flat shoes, and her bright black eyes were an inch or two below Sheila's own. It gave Sheila an odd feeling to look down on an adult. But the firm clasp of Kenny's hand and the warmth of her smile made Sheila feel sincerely welcome. "I hope you'll enjoy it here. We're certainly glad to have you."

"And this is Jerry Dressler." Willy introduced the other new student.

"Hello, Jerry." Jerry felt very tall as he shook her hand. She wasn't at all what he had expected. What *had* he expected? A silly eccentric with wild hair and dowdy clothes? Not this vibrant little woman. "It's always nice to greet a new boy—we've had a slight surplus of girls at our Saturday dances for three years." She looked around the room. "Where's Phillip Bruce?"

"He wasn't on the train," said Willy.

"Oh, he arrived just after you'd left with the bus; his parents drove him. I guess he's in his room and doesn't know dinner's served—the bell's out of order again. Mike, would you please go look for him? He's in your dormitory."

"Okay," said Mike and went off, his shoes clicking noisily on the worn linoleum; bits of gravel were sticking to the soles.

The interval before his return was enlivened by Sally's cat, which suddenly decided to attack somebody else's poodle and made a flying leap halfway across the room. For several minutes the black and brown fur flew—until Jerry resourcefully poured a jug of milk over the two, stopping the fight instantly. Sally apologized to the poodle's furious owner; the dog had gotten the worst of the fight.

"Now, please," Kenny said gently, "if you can't keep your pets under control, they'll have to be banished to the stable for the rest of the term. You all made that rule yourselves, remember?"

Mike came back into the room and shrugged his shoulders helplessly. "I couldn't find him."

"Oh, well, he'll be around somewhere. Thanks, Mike." Mike picked up an apple and bit into it with a loud crunch as Kenny went on. "Sheila, you'll be rooming with Mimi Holly and Sally Green." (Sheila's heart sank, thinking of the cat.) "Jerry, you and Phillip are in the big dorm." She gave Sheila and Jerry a warm smile. "You'll meet the rest of the teaching staff in your

17

classes. I'm sure everybody's in a hurry to go off and unpack right now. But first I've a few announcements which promise a good year.

"Gaby Newman has brought a Venus's-flytrap to replace that tired old rubber plant in the library. Pierre Cornay has a new movie camera and plans to make a film. Knowing Pierre, we can expect something experimental. And a rumor has reached my ears that Mimi Holly's written a play, which will be produced for next Saturday's entertainment." Mimi blushed. "Well, I guess that's all, unless Willy has anything."

"Just one thing," said Willy. "Please, I don't want any of you boys fooling around with my new electric razor. Most of you are far too young to shave anyway."

There were a few chuckles at this, then everyone began pouring out of the room. Sally hurried after Kenny. "Oh, Kenny— I've a problem with my cat. You see, Sheila is supposed to room with me and Mimi, and she's allergic to cats."

"Oh . . ." Kenny turned and looked at Sheila, a short distance behind. "I'm sorry, Sheila, I didn't know. The cat will have to sleep in the stable, then."

"But you *said* I could have him in my room," Sally protested. "He's *never* slept in a stable; he'll *hate* it! He's always slept on my bed, ever since he was a kitten—"

"I'm sorry, Sally—he'll just have to get used to it. He looks pretty tough to *me*."

"But . . . I brought everything for him—a scratching log and a new litter-box and three months' supply of cat litter—"

"Sally, that's just too bad. We're delighted to have pets here, you know that; but humans come first."

"But you *promised*—"

"Not another word, Sally, please."

Sally subsided, chewing her lip. She glowered at Sheila, who quickly looked away with the unpleasant feeling that she had already made an enemy.

The upstairs hallways were a chaotic tangle of opened, overflowing trunks and suitcases. In the room Sheila, Mimi, and Sally were to share, only Sally's things were in order. Her pretty blouses and many pairs of stretch pants hung in the wardrobe; her impeccable underwear was neatly folded in a drawer. She had brightened her bed with three small pink satin pillows. On the wall above hung a small oil painting, an abstract swirl of blues and greens.

"Sally's mother painted it—she's Michelle Perrault, the well-known painter," Mimi told Sheila (Sally didn't seem to be speaking to her this evening). "Sally's completely bilingual, lucky thing, since her mother's French and her father's English."

Sally had rather pointedly stacked several bags of the now useless cat litter in one corner as though to accuse Sheila; but they soon had to be moved back to her trunk in the hall, for Mimi discovered she was allergic to the stuff. "So you couldn't have had The Cat of Cats in here anyway," Mimi pointed out cheerfully, to try to pacify Sally. The atmosphere in the room was rather tense. But Sally stayed angry. "I could've used earth from the garden," she muttered savagely, brushing her long blond hair.

Most of the room was strewn with Mimi's possessions: the things she had carried on the train, masses of clothes, cotton blankets (because of her allergy to wool), several books, and a few ancient stuffed toys she couldn't bear to leave behind for fear that her mother would give them to her little sister for keeps. She had also monopolized the old marble fireplace. Along the mantel, in a neat line, were her six bottles of allergy pills and her mouse collection: cloth Beatrix Potter mice in little dresses, china and wooden mice, and a fluff-covered old candy one she'd been given years ago and couldn't bring herself to eat. "I love mice," she told Sheila; "they're so tiny and cute and delicate—everything I'd love to be and can't."

In contrast to Sally's decorations and Mimi's chaos, Sheila's own bed and dresser were very bleak and bare. Why hadn't she brought anything but clothes? she wondered suddenly. Why hadn't she thought of bringing her Mexican rug, her green glass vase, or her conch shell? Not having them there filled her with frustration. Well, she could write and ask Mother to send them. But she felt suddenly desperate to have something personal in this room, *now*. So she took the snapshot of her father from her wallet and fixed it inside the frame of her mirror. There—that was better.

"Gee," Mimi exclaimed, peering nosily, "who is that divinely handsome Older Man?"

"My father."

"Your lucky mother!"

"They're divorced."

"Did he remarry?"

"No."

"Well, then he's an eligible bachelor again."

"Yes, I guess so." Sheila had never thought of him in quite this way.

"Gee, I'd *love* to meet him. Sheila, get him to visit you and take us out to dinner—"

"He lives in Vancouver."

"Aw, gee! I'd just love to meet him. . . ." Mimi, not noted for tact, might have gone on in spite of Sheila's sullen, closed expression; but she was distracted by the sight of Sally in her underwear. "Sally! You're wearing a bra!"

"Just a thirty-two triple-A," Sally said modestly.

"Oh, it's not fair—you're only *twelve!* Gee, here I am, thirteen in August, already a teenager, practically six feet tall, and what have I got? Nothing! I tried to buy a bra once, but the salesgirl laughed at me."

The three were in pajamas when the door burst open. In came a small girl of ten or eleven, with thick black hair in a soup-bowl cut. "Hey, kids," she said breathlessly, "have you heard about the new boy? He nearly drowned—"

"You mean Jerry Dressler?" Sheila exclaimed.

"No, the mysterious one who never showed up. Phillip Bruce—at least he did show up, but he didn't come to dinner. Anyway, it turns out he went down to the river and took out the canoe and it capsized and he got caught in the current, but luckily somebody saw him and rescued him and brought him back and he's in the infirmary now but there's nothing wrong with him—"

Her breath gave out; she collapsed on Sally's bed. But before the others could speak, she jumped right up again. "I have to go tell the others. . . . Oh, there's a bedtime snack in the dining room for anybody who wants one—"

"Biscuits?" Sally asked hopefully as the small girl reached the door.

"No, apples, of course." And she was gone.

"That was Gaby," Mimi told Sheila. "Gee, this new boy sounds kind of wild."

"He's probably neurotic," said Sally, tying the sash of her blue-and-pink-striped dressing gown. "Well, I think I'll go get an apple." She went out.

"I bet she's really going because Ben Drexler will be there," Mimi said. "He's her steady boy friend—the one she was sitting with in the bus. Kind of cute, if you go for that pale, freckly type; I don't myself. They've been going steady for nearly a year."

"Oh." Sheila was impressed by Sally's sophistication.

Mimi's red-brown eyes narrowed curiously. "You know, that was pretty cool the way you used your allergy as an excuse to go and sit by that cute boy Jerry on the train. His type I *do* like."

"But I didn't," Sheila protested. "I mean, I did move to a different seat—but it was because of my allergy, my eyes were so watery I could hardly see—and that seat was the only other empty one—"

"Oh, come off it, Sheila. You didn't fool Sally and me for a minute, but it *was* pretty cool. I really go for that narrow-faced dark type. He's tall too, almost as tall as me."

"But . . ." Sheila gave up; she was obviously not going to convince Mimi. Anyway, Mimi seemed to rather admire her for it. Never, never could she admit to Mimi—and even less to Sally—that she hadn't yet had a date with a boy, not once, nor been to a dance. She'd felt new and strange with them all evening; now she felt embarrassingly young as well.

When they were finally in bed, after repeated nagging from one of the older girls, Sheila lay awake for a long time. She thought the other two were sound asleep, but Mimi whispered suddenly in the darkness, "If you feel homesick, go ahead and bawl—we won't mind; it's healthier than being brave. I cried for a week when I was new, though I love school now."

Sheila was rather touched by this, but she didn't feel like crying. The awful thing was, she hardly felt homesick at all. Since she couldn't be in Vancouver with Daddy, she'd almost rather be here than at home. I'll definitely send for my rug and vase and shell tomorrow, she decided suddenly, and finally fell asleep.

Chapter Three

*B*right sunlight shone through the tall, narrow windows. It fell upon Jerry's eyes as he rolled over in bed, and woke him up. Looking across the enormous, high-ceilinged room—which had once been the master bedroom—he saw a strange boy unpacking a suitcase near the door. In the other four cots the boys were still asleep. Mike's banjo lay on the floor, where he had left it after last night's noisy hootenanny. A large group of boys had gathered in the room, singing through mouthfuls of apple while Mike played. At one point some girls had tried to crash the party but were turned away firmly with the words "Strictly stag." The singing had continued boisterously till after ten, when Willy, reappearing for the third time, said if they didn't get to bed and shut up soon he'd . . . he'd . . . well, do something decisive. Willy, usually so amiable, was like a raging bull when he lost his temper. The boys were not intimidated by his threats, but shrugged tolerantly and decided they might as well go to bed. One by one the nine visitors dispersed to the other three smaller rooms in the boys' wing.

This particular boy had not been among them. He must be the mysterious Phillip Bruce. Half hiding his face under the blankets, Jerry watched Phillip silently.

He showed no signs of his recent ordeal in the river. Putting things in an open drawer, he walked stealthily, as though anxious not to wake anybody. Jerry had expected a rebellious oddball, but he didn't look it. He had short, wiry brown hair, blue eyes, and regular but rather pinched features. He was tall and muscular for his age—thirteen—and moved like an athlete. He wore khaki trousers and a gray sweatshirt.

Suddenly he looked around, as though instinctively, like a wary animal. He gazed at Jerry silently with suspicious blue eyes.

"Hi," said Jerry casually.

"Hi."

"I'm Jerry Dressler. Didn't hear you come in last night."

"Shhh—you'll wake them," Phillip whispered. "I came in just now."

"You all right?" Jerry asked uncertainly. They had all heard of Phillip's adventure with the canoe.

"Of course. Why shouldn't I be?" he said defensively. Jerry sensed that he wanted to pretend the whole incident had never happened—as though he were ashamed of it. Okay, then; that was all right with Jerry. But he wasn't so sure the other boys would shut up.

There was a loud hammering on the door.

"Breakfast, you guys," said a boy's voice. "The bell's out of order. There won't be a second warning."

The other boys awakened and began to drag themselves heavily out of bed—except Mike, who just went on snoring softly.

"Do we *have* to get up now?" Jerry asked. "I thought this school was supposed to be so free and all."

"Well, nobody will *make* you." Pierre's pale face was white with sleep. "But if you don't, you won't get any breakfast." He saw Phillip. "Well!" His eyes were teasing yet friendly. "The mysterious stranger!"

Phillip's mouth set in a tense line, but he said nothing.

"Well, hello, anyway." Pierre swung his legs over the side of the bed, stood up, and stretched. His fake blond mustache was slightly crooked. "I'm Pierre Cornay."

The others introduced themselves sleepily. Ian and Don were twelve; Pierre was fourteen, like Jerry; Mike (still asleep) was thirteen. Don gave Mike a fierce poke. "Come on, wake up and meet Phillip."

Mike's dark hair was rumpled, his face cross and sleepy. "Who are you?" he asked the new boy.

"Phil Bruce."

"Who?"

"*Phillip Bruce.*"

"Oh—him." Mike still looked cross and sleepy. "How did you get in here without waking us?"

Phil said nothing but went back to his unpacking. Pierre was at the mirror, gingerly adjusting his mustache. "Well, Phil," he remarked, in a light, friendly voice, "it seems you've begun your career at Kenner with a dramatic flourish, *mon ami.*"

Phil burst out, "I don't want to hear any more about it!" He stood for a moment glaring at them all. Then he stalked out. The door slammed behind him.

"Not a sociable type," Ian observed. Mike turned over heavily and went back to sleep.

"I don't know why he's so flustered," Pierre said amiably. "All he did was take out the canoe." Pierre pulled at his mustache, and winced painfully. "Oh, dear, I may be stuck with this thing permanently—it hurts too much to pull it off. And already I'm tired of it."

"Want me to give it a yank?" Jerry offered.

"Merci, non!"

Jerry went to a window, which looked down upon the remains of an elegant back lawn: several overgrown grassy slopes, then a wide stretch of mud, then the river. The water shone green and silver in the sun—a perfect Indian summer day. Pierre came and stood beside him, still fingering his mustache.

"That muddy part's our playing field. I imagine Liz Wright will be in one of her speedball moods today, with no classes. I'm not a keen player, but it's always fun the first day of term. You haven't met Liz, have you? She's a rather overpowering female."

"What's speedball?"

"Wait and see." Pierre's narrow yellow-green eyes sparkled humorously, and the other boys grinned.

Don gave Mike a second fierce poke. "Get up, you lazy blob. Speedball today!"

Breakfast was even more casual than dinner. You made your own toast at the big fireplace. There were eggs, milk and *café au lait,* and stewed apples. Everybody was eyeing Phil with curiosity, and many went up and spoke to him. Their manner was friendly enough, but he remained stiff.

Now that they were settled into school for the term, the students were dressed for comfort rather than elegance. The boys tended to favor jeans. Most of the girls wore tight slacks and loose jerseys; many had long, untidy hair which trailed in their food. Jerry noticed that even Sheila was wearing trousers this morning—no doubt following the others' example.

"Kenny would like to see Jerry, Sheila, and Phillip in the study after breakfast," Willy announced as he left the room.

Oh, yes, Jerry thought, now she was going to arrange the new students' courses. He remembered the typed sheet which the Kenners had sent his parents, listing an almost frightening variety of subjects:

TEACHING STAFF	COURSES
Miss Rosalie Dennis . . .	English Literature, Psychology, Comparative Religion, Sociology, Anthropology, and Greek Mythology
Mlle. Jeanne Dupont . . .	French, German, Modern Dance, and Singing
Mrs. William Kenner . . .	Chemistry, Biology, Botany, Geology, Mathematics, and Physics
Mr. William Kenner . . .	Canadian History, Modern European History, Geography, Economics, Philosophy, Political Science, Psychology of Politics in the Province of Quebec, Contemporary Canadian Politics, Carpentry, Handicrafts, First Aid, and others

Jerry found Sheila and Phil standing silently outside the door of the Kenners' study.

"Hi, Sheila," he said with his easy smile. "How goes it in the girls' dorm?"

"Hi!" She smiled back shyly. "Well, I have two roommates—Mimi Holly and Sally Green."

"I'm in a big room with five other guys."

"Oh. I'm lucky, I guess." She didn't sound as though she felt very lucky, somehow.

The door opened, and Willy came out. "All right; she'll see Phillip first." Phil went in, and Willy smiled at the other two. "If either of you is keen on taking Latin, I'll be only too glad to polish up my declensions."

From the twinkle in his eyes, Jerry gathered that this was

meant to be a joke: that nobody ever took Latin. And why not? he thought rather crossly. Any decent school should teach *some* Latin.

"Well, I must get to work," Willy said. "See you in class." He went away.

"How are your roommates?" Jerry asked Sheila.

"Mimi's very nice. How about yours?"

"They're okay."

A long silence fell. They leaned against the wall and shifted their feet. Jerry tried to listen to the conversation inside, but only a faint murmur emerged through the heavy door. Finally Phil came out. "Sheila's next," he muttered and hurried off.

The study, like so many rooms in the house, was large and shabby, with a high ceiling and a fireplace. The walls were brightened with colorful paintings. "Students' work," said Mrs. Kenner, who was seated in an armchair by the sunny window. "Sit down, will you, Sheila?" She smiled reassuringly, and Sheila sat on the chair facing her. "Kenny" was what everybody called Mrs. Kenner; but Sheila wasn't sure she could bring herself to address the headmistress by a nickname more suitable for a little boy. In the bright sunshine Kenny's brown skin looked rather coarse, her small, square hands work-worn; but her features were handsome and attractive.

"Well, Sheila, tell me what you're interested in."

Sheila, who had started to relax, stiffened again. Her mind went blank. Gee, what *was* she interested in? At her last school she had hated all her subjects or been bored by them and the teachers. But, gee, she must be interested in *something*. What's wrong with me, if I'm not interested in anything? Oh, I can't be interested in *nothing*, surely.

"I don't know," she said helplessly.

Kenny didn't seem at all dismayed by this. "You're not a keen student?"

"I'm afraid not."

"Not athletic?"

"No—I'm terrible at sports."

"Do you paint? Dance? Play the piano?"

"No." Sheila was feeling worse and worse. She must be a hopeless case.

"Do you sing?"

Sheila hesitated. At home, alone in the bathroom, she loved to sing. But that was just for fun, all by herself. That wouldn't count as a real interest—certainly not a talent.

"No," she said.

"Well, what do you do when you're all alone? Daydream?"

"Yes," Sheila confessed. "I daydream a lot."

"What do you daydream about? Or is it none of my business?"

Sheila thought of her "hate" daydreams, when she quivered with anger so fierce it almost frightened her; then she thought of her long, elaborate fantasies. Sometimes she was desperately alone—until a wonderful man came along who looked at her with new eyes, appreciating her as nobody ever had before; and she would look at him with the same understanding, seeing that under his independent surface he had always been lonely too. Sometimes she was a great singer, who gave joy to a vast audience or moved them to tears, and who was filled with love for all of them. Sometimes she was killed in a plane crash, and everyone mourned the death of one so young.

"It's none of your business," she said sullenly, uncertain how Kenny would react to this. But Kenny took it calmly.

"Do you ever write stories or poetry? Or a diary?"

"No, but I do read," Sheila exclaimed, happy at last to be able to describe something she was interested in. "I read a lot—adventure stories and historical novels—not children's books; most of them bore me."

"Good." Kenny smiled at her. "We have a fair-sized library up on the third floor—not a very selective collection, but certainly lots of books, all kinds. Get Mimi or somebody to show you where it is. And feel free to browse anytime and take books out. Since you enjoy reading, you might like to drop in on Rosalie Dennis's English class tomorrow and see if you want to take the course; it's very popular."

"All right." Sheila was feeling better already.

"Good. Now run along and send Jerry to me."

Sheila stood up, then paused uncertainly.

"What's the matter?"

"Nothing, but . . . is that all? I mean, what about French and math and so on?"

"Do you want to take them?"

"Well . . . not much."

"Not much, or not at all?"

"Not at all," said Sheila, growing bolder.

"Then what's the point of taking them? You wouldn't be much of an asset to the classes if you don't enjoy the subjects. Maybe you'll study them later on. But it's up to you completely."

Sheila left the room a little puzzled, a little uneasy. She didn't even have to go to the English class if she didn't want to. She could do whatever she liked. She could spend all her time reading books from the library . . . or just do nothing at all! "She'll see you now," Sheila told Jerry with a radiant smile, and hurried upstairs to her room, suddenly lighthearted. After all those dull subjects at her last school—the dreary routine, the nagging teachers—why, Kenner School was just too good to be true!

Neither Mimi nor Sally was in the room. She realized how quiet everything was. After the noisy chatter in the halls last night, the transistor radios blaring, this silence was almost un-earthly. Nobody seemed to be around. Where had they all gone? Looking out the window, which faced the front of the house, she saw Sally sitting on the steps (the paint must be dry by now, Sheila concluded) stroking her cat. Her voice came up faintly through the still, clear air. "Poor baby—did oo miss me? Did oo hate sleeping in that dirty old stable, like a common farm cat? Well, don't you worry, baby-puss—Mummy's going to visit you every day, and talk to you, and not let you be lonely. . . ."

Sheila moved away from the window. She sat down on her bed and looked around the room, which was rather large and square with dirty yellow walls. Aside from Sally's decorative touches and the mass of stuff piled on Mimi's bed, it looked very empty: just three narrow cots, three small chests of drawers—gray paint blistered—and an enormous oak wardrobe which reached to the ceiling. No doubt, Sheila thought, it would grow messy as the term wore on, for there was no housemother at Kenner and no room inspection.

She wondered what to do now. Could she find the library without Mimi's help? The house was easy to get lost in, with its confusing corridors and different levels. She looked at her new watch: only ten o'clock. Three hours till lunch, and she had nothing to do. She went to the window again. Sally and her cat were gone; there was nobody. The beauty of the day only made her feel more lonely.

The floor trembled suddenly as energetic footsteps came striding along the hall. A big blond girl appeared in the open doorway.

"Say . . . it's Sheila Davis, isn't it? What are you doing moping indoors on a beautiful day like this? Come down to the playing field, for heaven's sake. We're having a speedball game. Ever played speedball?"

"No." Sheila came forward eagerly, stirred into new life. She had never liked sports, but she welcomed something to do.

"Oh, you'll catch on. I'm Liz Wright, by the way." The big girl looked about fifteen. She wore yellow slacks and a blue shirt, buttons stretched to the breaking point over her large bosom. "Some hard running will do you good," she observed, eyeing Sheila as they left the room like a dealer sizing up a piece of horseflesh. "Loosen you up and work off your tensions with good healthy sweat. Got some nice bone on you but no muscle."

Liz continued to talk as they went along the corridor, Sheila almost running to keep up with the big girl's long strides. "I'm afraid speedball's really the only game we're equipped for this term. Winter is better; we can ski and skate. A couple of years ago we had a very athletic bunch of kids, and we made a tennis court on the front lawn; but it's all gone to pot. Unfortunately the school seems to be going through an artistic period right now. Art is all very well, but I think physical fitness is at *least* as important. . . ."

Sheila only half listened, following Liz breathlessly down the stairs and out the back door. They emerged into the warm sunshine behind the house. Before them a series of grassy slopes led down to the small, muddy playing field, where a large group of boys and girls were running around, kicking balls, wrestling, laughing, and screaming. The whole school seemed to be there. Sheila noticed Mimi, very leggy in tiny red shorts. Sally stood at the river's edge, watching the others.

"Now, just look at all that energy," Liz observed proudly, like a mother watching over an outsize brood. "All completely spontaneous! At what other school would you find so much completely free, spontaneous drive?" Sheila thought they looked much the same as any bunch of kids fooling around, but didn't say so. Liz took a tin whistle from her tight breast-pocket and blew a long, shrill blast.

Jerry entered the Kenners' study determined to put up with no progressive nonsense about expressing his personality. A headmistress called "Kenny" and a headmaster called "Willy" couldn't disguise the fact that basically this was just a school: a place you had to go to because your parents sent you.

"Well, Jerry," Kenny began, when he was seated, "tell me what you're interested in."

"Oh, lots of things," he said calmly. He had been expecting this kind of question and had his answer all ready. "I've studied French for two years, so I guess I'd better continue. I've studied some science but not chemistry; I'd like to take that this year. Do you have a good lab?"

She smiled. "I think you'll find it adequate. I teach chemistry myself. All the science labs are in the old stable."

"Well, I'd like to take it. And history. I feel I ought to know something about modern European history. And English, of course. And math. And . . ." Impulsively he burst out, "I'd like to take Latin."

"Latin?" She seemed surprised but rather pleased. "Have you studied it before?"

"No, I just thought I'd like to."

"Willy will be glad to have a Latin pupil; he enjoys variety. Now, you want to take French, math, chemistry, modern European history, English, and Latin. Isn't that rather a lot? You won't have much free time."

"It seems normal enough. Colleges expect you to have most of those subjects."

"You're anxious to go to college?"

"Yes, of course."

"Why?"

Her bright black eyes were fixed on his. It seemed important to his self-respect that he produce a good answer.

"Well, I think it's an essential opportunity to—to develop your mind. And you can't get anywhere without a degree."

"Yes, I'm afraid that's true nowadays." She looked at him thoughtfully. "Do you like sports?"

"Oh, yes—especially hockey."

"Fine—it's very popular here in winter. I hope you're comfortable enough in that big dorm, Jerry. I'm sorry about the lack of privacy, but so many of the rooms in this house are enormous, and we simply haven't the money to do much remodeling. But there are three student studies where you can work in peace and quiet."

"That's okay."

"Well, I guess you can go now. You'd better see the other teachers this afternoon and arrange a schedule."

"All right." Jerry started to go, then paused in the doorway. "What do I do now?"

"Why"—her smile was slightly teasing—"whatever you like!"

Jerry left the room feeling vaguely dissatisfied with the interview. Somehow he hadn't made a good impression. He wandered idly into the living room and played a few notes on the piano; it was out of tune. He sat irritably kicking at the pedals. What was he doing at this school, anyway? It was such a waste of time. Just because Dad had been to college with Willy Kenner: and because Dad and Mom were psychologists (*both* of them!) and felt a year at Kenner would be good for Jerry. Develop his personality or some such corny nonsense. Why couldn't they get it through their heads that all that progressive-school stuff was out of date?

He'd felt like such a fool telling his friends. "You mean that crazy coed place up in the wilds of French Canada?" they exclaimed incredulously. "Where kids go psycho and shoot their teachers?" (This was in reference to one such incident which had made the papers a couple of years ago.) They could hardly believe it: Jerry Dressler at Kenner School! It just wasn't his scene at all.

Not that the Kenner kids were so bad, now he was here. Mike and Pierre were okay. But if he must go to boarding school—which, in any case, would be a drag—he'd rather be at a regular one, rules and all.

Drawn by faint screams from outdoors, he rose and went to the window. Down by the river was a seething crowd of kids. Curious, he opened the door and went out. Just ahead of him he saw Sheila, standing beside a big blond girl. Oh, she must be the Liz whom Pierre had mentioned. Suddenly he was startled by an ear-splitting whistle.

"Okay, kids," the big girl boomed, "let's have a real game, eh? Okay. Now, what about teams? Boys and girls, or mixed?"

"Boys and girls!" several voices yelled from below.

"Okay. Sheila and I will go get the goal cages. You can help Sheila," she told Jerry, suddenly finding him there. "They're rather heavy."

Jerry remained standing as the two girls started in the direction of the stable. Liz looked back and stopped.

"What's the matter? Come on!"

Jerry said slowly, "Do my ears deceive me, or are we going to play this game boys against girls?"

"That's right," she replied amiably.

"How can we?"

"Why not? We usually play speedball that way. It's a good coed game."

"But—that's ridiculous!"

"Oh?" Liz's voice was cold now. "And just exactly what is so ridiculous about it?"

"There's no point to it; we'll win easily. If we must have a coed game, we should play with boys *and* girls on each team."

"What makes you so sure you'll win easily?"

Jerry spoke as though to a moron. "Because girls just happen to be made smaller and weaker than boys."

"Do *I* look small and weak?"

"Well—er—no. But what about—well, Sheila."

"She's not full-grown yet—give her time. How old are you, Sheila?"

"Thirteen in November."

"There!" Liz said triumphantly. "She's still a child."

Jerry glanced at Sheila. She dropped her eyes from his and shifted from one foot to the other, seeming slightly at a loss.

"Well, what about that girl—Sally?" Jerry persisted and gestured to where Sally was standing a little below, looking up with an amused grin at the argument. "Even if she lifted weights all day for years, you can't tell me *she'd* ever be a football type."

"I quite agree. But there's no reason why Sally couldn't be wiry and quick on her feet if she tried." Liz glared at Sally, who gazed back coolly, rather proud of not being athletic. "And this isn't football, it's speedball. We play many games mixed, but boys against girls is fun for a change. Enough of this talk—come on!"

Jerry was tempted not to follow; but in spite of his disgust with Liz's attitude, he was curious to see the game. He dragged one of the goal cages down the hill to the playing field, Sheila hanging on to one corner rather ineffectually. "Set it up here," Liz directed bossily as they raised it upright. Jerry gave Sheila a rueful grin, and she smiled back through the wire mesh. Not caring much for sports herself, she didn't mind that this game might be a farce. It would mean nobody caring much if she made a fool of herself.

"Good," Liz approved. "Now, for the benefit of you new kids, I'll explain the rules. Speedball is a combination of football, basketball, soccer, and field hockey. You use a basketball— Say, where is it, Ben?"

"We couldn't find it," a skinny freckled boy replied.

"Oh, well; we'll have to use the football, then. Anyway, you can kick *or* throw it, but you can't run with it. You have to keep throwing it up in the air and catching it. And you can't pick it up once it's on the ground. You get goals *and* touchdowns. Oh, somebody better mark the touchdown lines—thanks, Ben. Make sure they're even on both sides. . . . Well, you two better be goalies to begin with; you'll catch on after a while."

Jerry and Sheila set themselves up in their opposite positions. The positions of the other players were less definite, as the teams weren't even; there were seventeen girls and fifteen boys. Jerry was interested to see that Phil was present. He started the game with a powerful kickoff which sent the ball flying over Sheila's head and into the field beyond. "Out," said Liz, but she beamed at Phil approvingly. "With a kick like that and some practice, you should shape up well." They rescued the ball and put it in place for another kickoff. This time Mimi kicked it, with great energy, so that it flew sideways and into the river. There must have been a leak in it, for it sank like a stone. Somebody produced another ball—a small one, not designed for any specific sport—and they started again.

Now Tony, a tall, wiry boy of sixteen, kicked the ball. This time it flew only a few feet before Liz caught it and began to run, throwing it up in the air and catching it expertly. There was a great rush of excitement as she neared the boys' goal line.

Girls and boys hovered breathlessly around her, jumping up and down. *"Throw* it, Liz!" cried the girls. Liz flung the ball ahead, but Tony rushed forward and caught it just before it could cross the line. He threw it high in the air; Ben jumped for it and fell down; Mimi fell on top of him, long legs waving wildly.

Now Phil had the ball. He gave another of his magnificent kicks. It flew down the length of the field and sailed across the line, slightly to the left of Sheila, who made an ineffectual grab at the air.

"What's the *matter* with you?" Mimi yelled, her red shorts covered with mud. "You in a trance or something?"

"I'm sorry," said Sheila helplessly. "I wasn't quick enough."

"You hardly even *tried!*"

The ball was recovered and put in place for another kickoff. "Score: Boys, one; Girls, zero," Liz said efficiently. She blew her whistle; the game continued.

Jerry stood leaning against the back of his goal cage, arms folded. The faint, superior smile on his face showed what he thought of this boys-against-girls game. He simply would not take it seriously . . . Wham! Jerry started as the ball smashed against the wire, making the whole goal cage shake.

"I got a goal!" Mimi shrieked, jumping up and down excitedly. "I got a goal! For the first time in my life, I *scored!*"

"Good going, Mimi!" said Liz warmly. "Score, one even."

"The only reason she scored was because Jerry let her," said Mike, frowning at Jerry disgustedly. "He's as feeble as Sheila."

Jerry's face flushed in anger. Feeble as Sheila, indeed! This game was simply too much. It was beneath his dignity. He would quit now, simply walk away without a word. . . . But no, he couldn't. Not after letting Mimi (*Mimi,* who could hardly throw a ball straight!) get a goal so easily. He'd have to stay and show these kids what he could do. He stood in tense concentration, waiting for the next kickoff.

When they changed positions a little later, Jerry was the fastest runner on the boys' team. He got a goal and two touchdowns in quick succession; he earned loud cheers. Phil's grim, almost cruel kicks were still the most powerful; but his aim was weak. Sheila, running helplessly around the field, was even less of an asset to her team than before. She tripped, fell, got up, and continued running—confused, muddy, and miserable.

From time to time the game paused while players argued over the rules. Ben wanted to introduce tackling; most of the others were against it. But Liz listened to any suggestion, however silly, with respectful consideration. After two hours and the loss of another ball, everybody was exhausted. They went into lunch feeling ravenous. The boys had won, 23–19.

"An exciting game," Liz remarked to Sheila as they entered the dining room. "We Kennerites don't play too badly, do we?"

"I was awful," said Sheila, very subdued.

Liz looked at her quite kindly. "Do you like sports, Sheila?"

"No," said Sheila with sudden fierceness. "I hate them. Team sports, anyway, they bore me to death."

"Why didn't you say so before, then? If you really *hate* them, why play?"

"You mean . . . I don't have to?"

"Of course not," said Liz impatiently. Her expression was slightly disapproving but also tolerant. "Most of the kids here like sports, but not everyone. Sally and Pierre hardly ever play."

"Hey, Sheil!" Mimi waved from a nearby table. "Bring your food here, I've saved a seat for you. Gee, I *adore* your jeans," she added when Sheila joined her. "Did you fade them yourself?"

"Yes, I soaked them in bleach for three weeks," said Sheila, warmed by the compliment. She was proud of her jeans. They were so tight she could barely sit down.

Jerry and Mike stood at the sideboard, serving themselves from a pot of mysterious-looking stew.

"You must have a lot of problems playing baseball here," Jerry said. "I mean, with the river and all—you must lose a lot of balls."

"Oh, yeah. Baseball's pretty hopeless here. Hockey's okay, though."

"Boys-against-girls hockey?" Jerry asked sarcastically.

"No, mixed teams."

"But don't you ever have just boys playing against boys?"

"How can we? There aren't enough for two teams. Only fifteen boys in the whole school."

Jerry had no answer to that. Disgusted, he wandered over to Phil, who, a fast eater, was already back for dessert: baked apple. "Pretty silly game, don't you think?" he asked.

"Oh, all organized sports are ridiculous," Phil said impatiently. "Only thing I can say in favor of this dump is that they don't take sports too seriously."

He went off to a table, and Jerry sighed. Well, at least the boys' team had won: thank heaven for that. But if his friends at home could see him playing speedball against a bunch of girls!

Chapter Four

*A*fter dinner that evening Mimi took Sheila up to the library.

It was a large room filled with many shabby chairs. A battered dartboard hung on the door. There were also bookshelves, reaching to the ceiling; but little reading was done here after dinner. "The library is our favorite evening hangout," Mimi said as they entered the room, which was full of students. "We toast marshmallows and plan our weekly entertainments. Most important is Sunday night. Then the whole school meets here to discuss school affairs. Nobody *has* to come, of course, but most do; it's fun."

"The whole school?" Sheila looked around the room. Today was Sunday, but she couldn't see any teachers present. "What about the teachers?"

"Oh, tonight they'll be too busy—planning their schedules for the term." Mimi frowned. "I don't see that cute boy Jerry anywhere, do you?"

"No. Nor Phillip."

But everyone else seemed to be there. A large group was gathered around a small table, admiring Gaby Newman's Venus's-flytrap and feeding it flies. Pierre had christened the plant "Louise."

"Come on, kids," urged Dick, a fat blond boy of about fourteen. "It's time we started electing the officers for the term. I propose Mike as library officer."

"*Mike?*" Mimi exclaimed. "But he never reads a book if he can help it! You can't have a nonreader as librarian; it wouldn't be right."

"I don't want the job, anyway," said Mike firmly.

"Okay, okay," said Dick. "It was just a suggestion."

His proposal, however inappropriate, had at least broken the ice. Other candidates were suggested: Sally, Pierre, and a pretty girl called Rachel. Everybody voted by raising their hands, and Rachel won.

"Okay," she said, immediately inspired by her new position, "I propose a new rule: only three books out at a time per person."

"Why only three?" Pierre objected. "Let's say five."

"Four," said Gaby.

"One," said Mike.

"I think *any* rule about the number of books you can take out is just silly," said Dick.

They argued the matter heatedly for some time. Rachel's proposal was finally turned down by popular vote.

"Are we allowed to make up our own rules?" Sheila asked. She was perched on the window seat, nursing a sore arm. That afternoon a doctor from the village had come to give everyone typhoid shots so they could swim in the river (noted for its pollution). "Don't the Kenners make the rules?"

"Oh, no!" Mimi exclaimed, as though shocked by the very idea. "*We* make our rules. Of course the Kenners can sug*gest* rules if they like," she conceded, "but we have to approve them by popular vote."

"Well, they can vote too, of course," Ian added. "And the teachers."

Sheila still couldn't quite believe it. "What if you vote for something they don't like? Like—well, say, no bedtime rule at all?"

"Oh, we did that once. They weren't pleased, but we went ahead anyway. After a few nights of noise and not much sleep, most of us decided we pre*ferred* a bedtime rule."

"I propose a new office this year," Pierre broke in. "Somebody to keep track of all the supplies in the art studio. Last year everything got muddled, and we never knew when to order more paint. I wouldn't object to the job myself," he offered modestly.

"Oh, gee, can't that wait till later?" Mimi pleaded. "We always spend so long discussing every proposal, and I haven't even cast my play yet! We've less than a week for rehearsing and learning lines."

"Okay, Meem," said Sally. "Is there a part for me?"

"Of course—but you don't have any lines; I hope you don't mind. You're a cat, so you just meow. Later you turn into an elephant. Everybody turns into elephants at the end—that's done through acting, of course; the costumes would be too big."

Mike began lumbering elephantlike around the room, waving an imaginary trunk and trumpeting loudly; everyone but Mimi roared with laughter. Sheila tried not to, out of consideration for Mimi, who looked ready to burst into tears of frustration; but Mike really was very funny.

He finally sat down, and Mimi went on.

"It's called *Nothingness*," she said, her voice trembling with anxiety. Now that the moment of her debut as a playwright was at hand, she was terrified they might not like it. The reactions of Kenner students were unpredictable and apt to be extreme. They could be wildly enthusiastic or withering in their scorn. They were seldom merely polite.

43

"It's a theater-of-the-absurd play," she went on. "Which means it *seems* silly and nonsensical, but deep down it means something. Even *I* can't tell you just what it means, because I didn't think it out before I wrote it—I just let myself go. The meaning comes from my sub*conscious*. Rosalie says all great art comes from the subconscious."

"Okay, okay," said Mike impatiently. "Never mind your subconscious. What about the *play?*"

Mimi continued, warming to the subject now that she definitely had everybody's attention.

"There's this man—you're him, Pierre—an old man with a beard who lives in a garbage pail and doesn't communicate with anybody. He talks in rhymes. Lots of people come to see him and talk, but nothing makes much sense and nobody can communicate. There's a cat who meows—Sally—and a man and wife who don't know each other—Dick and Rachel. I mean, the *audience* knows they're married, but they don't recognize each other. And they have a little daughter—Gaby—who doesn't recognize them either, and they don't recognize her. Then there's an old bum who's drunk all the time—that's you, Mike. And a glamorous movie star in a red dress—I thought I might try that part; I have a new dress that's just right for it. Oh, and there's also a girl with a green face who keeps coming on and singing French Christmas carols. You can be her, Sheila," she said kindly.

"But"—Sheila was startled—"I'm not a singer . . . I mean—"

"I don't *want* an especially good singer. If I did, I would have given that part to Sally; she sings divinely."

Squashed, Sheila subsided, and Mimi went on. "Anyway, they talk and talk but still can't communicate. It isn't just tragic, of course; there are lots of funny lines. At least there should be— maybe somebody can think of some good jokes to stick in. But finally they all turn into elephants and stampede away. The old man doesn't, but he's lonely, so he gets out of the garbage pail and brings in a lot of chairs and pretends they're people. Then he hears an air-raid siren and gets back in his garbage pail and puts on the lid. A bomb falls, and it's the end of the world. Then the girl with the green face comes on in a spotlight, dressed as an angel and playing a banjo, and she sings 'I'll See You in My Dreams.' "

There was a long pause. Sheila didn't know what to say; it sounded such complete nonsense. Mimi clutched the script tightly, trying to keep her hands from trembling. She didn't dare look at anybody.

"Well, Mimi," Dick said finally, "it's difficult to judge before we've actually read the lines. But are you sure you know what you're doing?"

"Dick just means it's not quite like any other plays we've done," Rachel put in tactfully. "It's so different from Ellen's comedies and Bill's murder mystery. But it should be fun to act."

"Wonderfully theatrical," Pierre added.

"You like it, then?" Mimi exclaimed in relief. "Oh, I'm so glad! I think an angel playing a banjo's kind of a good touch, don't you?"

"It's great, Meem," Sally decided. "But awfully gloomy. Couldn't you make the ending a bit happier for that poor old man?"

"But it *is* happy," Gaby protested. "They all go to heaven."

"They *don't*," said Mimi indignantly.

"The girl with the green face does."

"She *doesn't*. You didn't understand—that's meant to be sa*tirical*. Oh, you've all missed the point entirely!"

Sally finally calmed her down. Dick said, "The bomb is going to be a rather difficult piece of stage business." Dick was a practical type.

"I thought we could make it just sort of symbolic."

"Something outrageously theatrical," Pierre suggested. "Like having somebody lower a black ball with *Bomb* written on it in white letters—lower it on a string. That would make the ending grim *and* funny at the same time—what's called a 'black comedy.'"

"Yes!" Mimi's face was radiant. "That's it *exactly*, Pierre. Maybe your new roommate Jerry might like to handle the bomb."

"I'll ask him."

Sheila was brooding about the epilogue. It was odd that Mimi should have hit upon that particular song for her to sing. There were very few songs like that. Sheila couldn't say what there was about them that gave her this special feeling, but "I'll See You in My Dreams" was one. She loved to sing it alone. But singing one of her special songs in front of a crowd might be worse than just any old song. "Mimi, I can't play the banjo," she protested.

"Well, fake it, then."

"I can teach you the chords for that song," Mike offered kindly. "They're very easy."

"All right," said Sheila. "Thanks." She had been in school plays twice before, but only as a walk-on. Nobody had ever considered her for a proper part, and she had never asked to try for one. Now, at the thought of this part, she was apprehensive yet excited. She was grateful to Mimi and Mike for not letting her wriggle out of it.

"Well," said Mimi, "you can borrow the script first, Pierre. Of course this is only kind of a rough draft, because I want everybody to feel free to add lines and improvise so it'll be *fresh* and spon*taneous*. In some places I've just put 'funny line' or 'nonsense line,' and you make one up." She handed Pierre a thin sheaf of papers. "Remember, all yours have to be in rhyme."

Jerry was lying on his bed reading a murder mystery when Mike and Pierre returned to the dormitory an hour later. "Hey, Jerry," said Mike, "why didn't you come to the meeting? You missed hearing Mimi describe her play."

"I just didn't feel like it," said Jerry almost sulkily. He had been in an aloof, superior mood ever since the speedball game that morning.

"Where's Phil?"

"Dunno. Haven't seen him since dinner." Suddenly Jerry was sorry he hadn't gone to the meeting. It might have been fun. "What's Mimi's play about?" he asked curiously.

"*Nothingness.*" Pierre handed him the script, and Jerry read the opening page:

> *Scene: A bare stage except for a garbage pail with the lid off. An old man with a beard sticks his head up. He speaks in rhymes. Nothing he says makes much sense. Enter a cat. The cat meows. Enter a man.*
>
> MAN: How brightly the sun shines! I think I'll go get a suntan.
>
> OLD MAN: Rain, rain go away, come again another day.
>
> MAN (reading newspaper): Dear, dear—another up-rising in Transylvania. I wonder if the stock market will go up or down this time?
>
> OLD MAN: Come and drown with me in the deep blue sea, so very very very very very merrily.
>
> CAT: Meow.

MAN: What a nice friendly dog! Here, Fido, good boy, Fido.

CAT: Purrrrrrrrrrrrrrrrrrr!

OLD MAN: Mice are nice. Cats are bats. Dogs are hogs.

(They go on talking nonsensically for a while. Enter a LITTLE GIRL.)

LITTLE GIRL: I'm lotht. Will thomebody pleathe help me find my way home? Boo-hoo.

MAN: It's time for all good little boys to be in bed. Ha-ha.

(They talk some more.)

Jerry stopped reading. "You know, this play seems kind of lacking in dialogue."

"We're supposed to improvise," said Pierre. "I'm the old man and Mike is a drunken bum. And Mimi would like you to help with a bit of business at the end." He explained about the bomb. Jerry was dubious.

"The whole thing sounds awfully silly."

"Of course it is. Even Mimi knows it's silly, deep down. But it might be entertaining."

"Oh, all right, then," Jerry said amiably. "I guess it'll be a few laughs." He smiled at the other two boys, cheering up suddenly. Maybe a year in this place wouldn't be so bad. Surely he could survive one year.

"First rehearsal in the stable loft tomorrow after breakfast," Mike announced. He had already taken over the directing from Mimi, who had lots of ideas but lacked authority.

"What about English class?" said Pierre.

"Well, then—say after lunch." Mike went to the windows. "Gee, I hope this hot weather keeps up so we can swim when our shots have taken."

Pierre looked glum. "I wish *I* could swim." He wasn't allowed to because of his asthma.

"Oh, you're not missing much, really. The river's muddy and full of leeches," Mike told Jerry.

"It's still wet," said Pierre, who loved water. "I'm thinking of making my film about some people who drown and are reborn as fish. But it will be difficult technically." He had finally pulled off his mustache, and his upper lip was pink and sore-looking.

The door opened, and Phil appeared.

"Hello! Where have you been?" Jerry asked pleasantly.

"Out."

"Another canoe trip?" Mike quipped.

"I went for a *walk,* for heaven's sake! Any crime in that?" Phil's scowl was so fierce, Mike flinched a little.

"Mimi Holly's written a crazy play for next Saturday," Pierre said, trying to be friendly.

"Oh," said Phil. He picked up a magazine from under his bed—*True Adventures*—lay down, and began to read.

Rosalie Dennis was the youngest of the teachers and newest to the school. "She and I were new together, two years ago," Mimi told Sheila, "and we've kind of developed together. She was sort of shy at first, but you'd never guess it now."

No, I wouldn't, Sheila thought. The English teacher, blond and pretty, dressed in neat blue slacks and a white blouse, had a cool self-possession rather like Sally's, but more aggressive. "We all call her Rosalie," Mimi added as they sat down. "Isn't Rosalie a *darling* name?"

There were fifteen students present, for English was a popular course. (Many classes had only two or three students.) They varied in age from little Gaby, who was eleven and looked younger, to tall dark Tony, who was sixteen. They sat upon a variety of ancient chairs in a crowded sitting room which didn't at all resemble a classroom. Rosalie Dennis sat on a small sofa, leaning back against the cushions and slowly swinging one foot, as though keeping time to some distant music only she could hear.

"Well, now, what would you like to read this term?"

There was an immediate clamor of voices. Rosalie waved her hand with a little smile. "Please, please—not all at once. What's your suggestion, Mike?"

Mike, who hadn't been one of the ones talking (he'd been gazing out the window), started but recovered himself quickly.

"Shakespeare?"

"Not a bad idea. We've never read any Shakespeare, have we? Which play?"

"Um—*Hamlet?*"

"Oh, *Hamlet's* full of long boring soliloquies," Dick objected. "Let's choose something with more action in it. *King Lear?*"

"*Julius Caesar,*" said somebody else; "*Macbeth*"; "*Othello*"; and Gaby piped up from the back of the room, "What about *Titus Andronicus?* I hear it's full of murders. Daddy acted in it once, but he wouldn't let me go and see it."

"Let's vote," said Rosalie. "Hands up for *Hamlet* . . . *Lear* . . . *Julius Caesar* . . . *Othello* . . . *Macbeth* . . . *Titus* . . ."

Hamlet won, to Dick's disgust. *Titus Andronicus* sounded intriguing, but several people had seen the movie of *Hamlet* and felt it would be easier.

"*Hamlet* it is, then." Rosalie looked at Mimi, who was almost bursting with something to say. "Well, Mimi, do you have a suggestion?"

"It's the Bible," said Mimi earnestly. "I think we ought to know more about the Bible. The Bible is the most famous book in the world. Being a cultured person means knowing the Bible. I read somewhere that kids today don't know nearly enough about the Bible."

"Hands up for the Bible," said Rosalie. No hands were raised. Mimi looked hurt.

"Never mind, Mimi—it was a very good idea. Now, why don't you do a study of the Bible on your own and give a talk on it to the class? I'm sure we'd all find that very interesting."

"The whole thing?" Mimi asked plaintively.

"Not unless you want to. Choose whatever most interests you." She gave her a smile so dazzling that Mimi, inspired, resolved to try and read the whole book.

"Well, now, that's only *Hamlet* so far. What about something modern?"

"Beat poets!" said Ben eagerly.

"But we read so many of them last year, Ben."

"Well, what about *Finnegans Wake?* It's supposed to be James Joyce's most far-out book. It's all written in the subconscious or something."

"Really?" Mimi exclaimed. "Gee, it must be a fabulous book."

After a brief argument it was generally agreed that *Finnegans Wake* would be interesting to sample.

"We may not get very far," Rosalie warned, "but we'll give it a darn good try. Now, what about some poetry?"

"Coleridge?" said Jerry.

"Ogden Nash," said Dick. Ogden Nash won by a large majority.

"Well, that's a nicely varied selection." Rosalie smiled approvingly. "Jerry, why don't you read some of Coleridge on your own and give us a talk? Well, now, let's have somebody tell us a story."

"I know a great story," Mimi began, but everyone shouted her down.

"Sally! Let Sally tell us one!" So Sally moved over to the sofa beside Rosalie and told a ghost story. Her voice was quiet, undramatic, yet somehow spellbinding. The others felt shivers run up and down their spines in spite of the bright, unghostly sunlight in the room. Everyone applauded when Sally finished. But then Gaby burst into tears.

"Oh, dear, oh, dear, oh, gosh—now I'm going to have night-mares for weeks! Every time I hear a new ghost story, I take weeks to get over it."

"You weren't scared by my murder mystery," Ben pointed out.

"Murders don't scare me, only ghosts. . . ." She cried so loudly that Rosalie asked Mimi to take her for a walk in the sunny garden. After they had gone, she told the others about the theory that Shakespeare didn't really write his plays, and who might have. They all found this interesting.

"So go off now and read *Hamlet*," she concluded. "When you've all read it, which I hope won't take *too* long, we'll meet again and discuss it and act out scenes." The class rose. "Oh, I'd like you new ones to stay behind a minute, please." Sheila and Jerry remained. (Phil wasn't taking English.)

"Wait outside a minute, Jerry, will you? I want to talk to each of you alone."

When he had gone, Rosalie patted the sofa beside her for Sheila to sit down. She reached into a purse, took out a pair of slanting glasses, and put them on; they gave her a Siamese cat look. She stared at Sheila penetratingly for a moment, as though seeing straight through her. Then she flashed her a sudden dazzling smile, then looked serious.

"I know you resent being here, Sheila, and I understand

perfectly. You feel your mother and stepfather are getting rid of you. Well, you know something, Sheila? You're quite right. They *are*."

Sheila was too startled to feel resentful. She was speechless.

"You hate them for this, of course, and you feel guilty for hating them. But don't torment yourself with guilt, Sheila. Believe me, your resentment is normal. Any child in your position feels the same way." She picked up a book from the table. "I suggest you go and read this. You'll be relieved to know how normal you are." Sheila looked at the title. *Children and Divorce: 100 Case Histories.* "And maybe you'd like to join my psychology class at eleven-thirty?"

"I'm not interested in psychology," said Sheila sullenly.

"Oh, yes, you are, Sheila. Everybody's interested in psychology. You're just afraid of it, that's all." She smiled gently. "Enjoy the book. And *Hamlet* too."

Jerry grinned at Sheila when she came out. "This scene is getting kind of familiar."

"Watch out for her," Sheila whispered. "She wants to psychoanalyze us or something."

"Oh, don't worry; I can handle *that*. My parents are psychologists—*both* of them. I've been analyzed all my life."

He entered the room feeling smug.

"Well"—Rosalie smiled at him—"you seem a very self-assured young man. But rather conventional in your tastes, I suspect. Do you resent your parents for sending you here?"

He paused a moment, then said daringly, "I suppose you have a Ph.D. in psychology?"

Her smile vanished. "Why do you suppose that?"

He wondered if he'd gone too far, but it was too late to turn back now. "Because otherwise you're not really qualified to analyze people you hardly know," he said uncomfortably.

For a long, horrible moment she stared back icily. He couldn't meet her steely gaze; he dropped his eyes. Then she smiled stiffly.

"Well, Jerry, you've really got me there! I'm afraid I have just a General Arts B.A. All right—run along. And have fun with *Hamlet*."

At lunch Pierre asked Sheila how she liked Rosalie.

"Well, she's a very interesting teacher. But—kind of nosy."

He chuckled. "Yes, we've all had that. Let me give you a warning: *Don't* take her psychology course; she's far worse in it."

"But—it's a wonderful course!" Mimi exclaimed indignantly. "We tell her our dreams," she informed Sheila, "and she helps us analyze them. And she asks us questions about our families, and we give each other tests—ink blots and word associations, and all kinds of fascinating things; and we analyze them. And, gee, I *never* would have known my twenty-two allergies are psycho—psychoso*matic* till she told me! She's given me so much *insight* into myself."

"But she's so—so *glib*," Pierre objected.

"It's bad for an amateur to try and analyze people," Jerry said knowingly. "Even my parents don't mess around with human beings. They stick to rats—it's safer. I guess I count as a rat, since I'm their son." Everybody laughed.

"Are all the teachers like Rosalie?" Sheila asked.

"Oh, no, they're all very different," said Tony. "Kenny's inspiring, and Jeanne is critical, and Willy knows a lot—he can teach anything. Even Psychology of Politics in the Province of Quebec. Oh, Willy, I wish *you'd* teach Psychology this year," he added as Willy sat down at their table with a bowl of soup.

"Afraid I'm too busy," said Willy. He looked at Sheila with a little frown. "Has Rosie Dennis been asking any awkward questions?"

"Well . . ."

"Kenny and I must speak to her about that. Don't let it bother you."

"What's the *matter* with you people?" Mimi frowned in distress. "You don't want Rosalie to *leave,* do you?"

"Oh, no," said Sally. "We all love our Rosie, except when she's nosy." Everybody but Mimi laughed. Sally's bright blue eyes turned suddenly upon Sheila. "Remember, on the train, I mentioned I didn't adore Rosalie the way Mimi does? Well, now you know why." It was the first time since that train journey that Sally had spoken to her.

PROGRAMME OF ENTERTAINMENT
Saturday, September 11, 7:30 P.M.

1) A Medley of Original Folk Songs for Banjo and Flute

Banjo—Michael Fraser
Flute—Janet Hale

Songs composed by Michael Fraser

2) NOTHINGNESS

A Black Comedy in One Act

by Emily Holly

CAST

OLD MAN . . . . Pierre Cornay
CAT . . . . Sally Green
MAN . . . . Richard Bardolis
LITTLE GIRL . . . . . Gabrielle Newman
WOMAN . . . . Rachel Robinson
MOVIE STAR . . . . . . Emily Holly
BUM . . . . Michael Fraser
GREEN-FACED GIRL . . . Sheila Davis

Costumes—Rachel Robinson
Lighting—Janet Hale
Special Effect—Gerald Dressler

Time: Anytime
Place: Anyplace

3) Dancing in the Dining Room

Disk jockeys: Janet Hale, Richard Bardolis
Refreshments: cocoa and apples

Time: after the play,
till the Kenners send us to bed

Chapter Five

. . . My story has a moral,
   And it is plainly this:
Oh, when you date a pretty girl,
   Be sure to get a kiss.

If you don't, she won't respect you,
   She'll leave you very soon,
So kiss your girl and dance till dawn,
   Under the light of the moon.

*M*ike's last song ended, and loud applause filled the living room. The flute and banjo didn't really harmonize as well as he'd hoped, but the songs themselves were a success. Janet, a pale, plump girl, rose to take a bow with him. Then Mike went off to change for the play. Janet joined the audience, which was composed of all twenty-three students not in the production plus the staff. This was the first Saturday entertainment of the term—exactly a week since the students had arrived at Kenner.

Heavy green curtains hid one end of the room, which was used as a stage for school productions. There was a pause of about twenty minutes; the audience grew restless and bored. Finally the big overhead light went off, and the curtains began to open. As usual they stuck halfway. While Ben unstuck them, the audience peered at the garbage pail revealed through the gap. "Ah, so *that* is what 'appen to it," Madame murmured to Mildred Hobbs, the school nurse.

"I only hope they disinfected it," Mildred whispered in reply. "I've a strong feeling there's somebody inside." The curtains opened all the way; the performance began.

It began very well. Pierre's appearance, in a long gray beard, earned a loud roar of applause. So did Sally as the cat—black leotard, pointed cardboard ears, wire whiskers, cloth-covered wire tail. The audience laughed at all the opening lines. Mimi, standing breathlessly in the large cupboard which served for off-stage, relaxed a little. Good, oh, good, they were enjoying it. But her palms sweated so much she was afraid of staining her red silk dress.

Sheila's first entrance was after Gaby. Mimi had meant Sheila to enter "spontaneously," whenever it seemed like a good idea; but Mike insisted on giving her definite cues. This was lucky, for otherwise she might never have gotten up the nerve to go on at all. Instinctively she sensed she would be most effective as a contrast to the dramatic posturings of the others. Acting before an audience was so different from rehearsing in the stables; you suddenly sensed the audience being bored, and realized a change of pace was needed to keep their interest. So when her cue came, Sheila walked quietly to the front of the stage, folded her hands, and sang in a low, breathless voice:

> Il est né, le Divin Enfant,
> Jouez, hautbois! Résonnez, musettes,
> Il est né, le Divin Enfant,
> Chantons tous son événement.

The audience chuckled delightedly. Standing there so primly in her white dress, hair in two bunches sticking out at each side, Sheila looked like a green-faced doll. Exiting as primly as she had entered, warmed by their response, she too realized suddenly that she had had the effect of an absurd doll. As she returned to the cupboard she resolved to play up this aspect throughout the performance. She hadn't during rehearsals; but Mimi had urged everyone to improvise, hadn't she? Well, then, Sheila would be a doll. A *clockwork* doll! she thought, suddenly inspired as she stood wedged in the cupboard between Mike and Rachel. A doll which, when wound up, went on stage, sang "Il est né, le Divin Enfant" very mechanically, and went off. Before, she had sung a different carol for each entrance, and spent some time learning all the words. Now she knew it would be more effective to stick to the same one.

The performance went on, but the audience's interest flagged. There were many awkward pauses while the actors frantically tried to think of something nonsensical to say. Even well-rehearsed lines began to earn rather half-hearted chuckles. Mike's appearance as a drunken bum, in an old coat and hat of Willy's, was a brief bright spot. Mimi as the movie star was not a success. Her entrance was somewhat impressive, in the red dress—a flapperish garment with a fringe around the hips—tottering unsteadily on her heels. But when the audience laughed at her, it wasn't amused laughter; it was slightly scornful. The elephant stampede was the biggest failure of all. Most of the audience didn't even realize the actors were meant to be elephants.

But Sheila was a hit. Every time she came on, the audience laughed more loudly. She had five entrances altogether—not including the final one. Each time she sang just a little more slowly and softly, as though her machinery were wearing out. Her arms and legs grew stiff and creaky; her eyes were glassy. Upon her fifth entrance she had a final inspiration: she opened and closed her mouth, and no sound came out. Then, very, very slowly, she went off—just barely making it. The audience roared and clapped.

Jerry was standing on a tall stool behind the curtain. Now, stretching out an arm, he lowered the bomb slowly on its string. It was a large beach ball, painted black, with B O M B in big white letters. Unfortunately it turned around, and the letters didn't show. The audience, having just heard Dick's ear-splitting siren imitation, got the idea; but coming so soon after Sheila, the bomb effect fell rather flat.

Suddenly they were plunged into darkness. Thinking it was over, they started uncertainly to clap, then fell silent as Janet shone a flashlight on the stage. Sheila entered once more, hair loose on her shoulders, silver cardboard wings pinned to her dress. Her face was still green. She discovered she couldn't see the banjo well enough to play the chords Mike had taught her; so she just held it and sang "I'll See You in My Dreams." No longer was she a mechanical doll; she was a wistful, green-faced angel, singing farewell to the world.

Loud clapping, stamping, and cheering filled the room. Mimi slipped away while the other actors were still taking bows.

"Sheila, you were *great!*" Mike didn't seem to mind that she had disobeyed most of his direction. "You *made* the show."

Sheila was surrounded by congratulations.

"*Fabulous*, Sheila!"

"I nearly *died* laughing. . . ."

"Your song at the end . . ."

". . . hilarious . . ."

". . . inspired . . ."

". . . star quality . . ."

Sheila leaped up the stairs like a gazelle. She couldn't remember having ever been so happy. She skipped into her room to remove her green make-up for the dance—and found Mimi lying on her bed in the dark, sobbing.

"Mimi! What is it?"

"Go 'way! Leave me alone— Ohhhh, I'll never write another play! What a dismal flop!"

"Mimi, it wasn't." Sheila tried to comfort her, although she had gotten the impression herself that the play as a whole wasn't a great success. "Didn't you hear the applause?"

"That was for *you,* not the play. You were a success, but the play was a ghastly flop. And I was the biggest flop of all! Oh, go away! Get out! Leave me alone!"

Slightly subdued, Sheila went to the bathroom and removed most of the green makeup. She still looked a little sickly, but her eyes shone. In spite of Mimi's misery, she couldn't help still feeling selfishly happy. Nothing could depress her tonight.

The dining room was filled with loud music from the phonograph. Tables and benches were pulled back against the colorful walls. Sally and Ben were dancing, while the others wandered around, drinking cocoa, munching apples, laughing and talking. Overhearing various conversations, Sheila realized the play hadn't been a complete flop after all. The audience praised a number of small touches, and hoped Mimi would go on writing.

Gradually the others began to dance—including Willy, to help make up for the slight shortage of boys. Sheila didn't sit out once. She was the heroine of the evening; she danced with everybody. At first she was a little worried about never having learned to dance, but she soon found it didn't matter. Some of the boys couldn't either; they just walked or bounced around in time with the music. Others danced very well but oddly, doing unpredictable steps which even a far better dancer than Sheila could hardly have followed. However, they didn't mind her ineptitude; they stamped and whirled by themselves, now and then flashing her a friendly smile in recognition that she was still their partner.

It was a relief to dance with Jerry, who was smooth and easy to follow. Whirling in his arms, Sheila overheard a scrap of conversation between Mike and Rachel nearby. "But if one gets you in a really dangerous grip," Mike was saying, "don't struggle—they just squeeze tighter. Tickle them under the chin—they love it; their muscles go all loose and they let go."

"What on earth is he talking about?" Sheila asked.

"Pythons," said Jerry, "or boa constrictors," and they laughed breathlessly.

If Sheila was the heroine of the evening, Sally was the sweetheart. She had been appealingly feline as the cat; and, anyway, Sally was always popular with the boys. There were other pretty girls present, but Sally had a special magnetism all her own. Smiling or sober, friendly or aloof, dancing or still, Sally attracted boys. She reserved every fifth dance or so for Ben; in between she danced with everybody. She was a beautiful dancer, graceful and gay. Her cheeks were flushed, her eyes shone like sapphires.

Mimi reappeared at last. She still wore her red dress, but with flat shoes, because of the boys. She seemed completely recovered from her gloom.

"You were *wonderful*, Sheila!" she exclaimed as though they hadn't met in the bedroom earlier. "Sally and I are proud to have such a talented roommate."

"I doubt if Sally's so proud." Sheila frowned resentfully when she thought of Sally, who deigned to recognize her existence these days but was still distinctly cool. Why did her single allergy have to be toward cats? She almost envied Mimi her twenty-two different ones. But she was puzzled by Sally, as well as irritated. She could see why the boys went for her, she was so pretty; but why did she seem to be so popular with the girls as well? She was often so aloof—even to Mimi, her best friend.

"You don't appreciate Sally yet," Mimi was saying. "She's not nice to you because of the cat, so you don't realize how great she is when she *is* nice. It's not that she isn't selfish. She often *is* selfish. But Sally's special. I guess I'm pretty popular in the school by now myself," she said modestly. "I'm in*volved* in lots of things; I know my way around. That's why the Kenners thought it'd be a good idea for you to room with me, since I'm not exactly the shy type. But I have to *work* at it; I have to *do* things—so do Mike and Pierre. And most people. Sally doesn't have to work at it. I can't explain it, but she's just special."

Sheila couldn't agree with this; but right now she didn't care. She was dancing with Jerry again. Mimi danced twice with Phil. "Well, at least he's tall," she said afterward, trying to be kind. "But what a *pill*." And so a new nickname was born: Phil the Pill.

To wind up the evening, Mike took up his banjo again and asked Sally to sing some folk-song solos. In her usual coolly self-possessed way, she agreed. She stood in her blue-and-green-striped shirt and green slacks, hands folded, while he sat on a chair beside her and played. Her voice was high, thin, very sweet and clear. It made even a cheerful ballad slightly wistful. Listening, Sheila was a bit envious. She knew she could never sing like that. She was still happy, but she no longer felt like the only heroine of the evening.

Chapter Six

*A*fter that wonderful evening, somehow life went steadily downhill for Sheila, all through the term. For a few days she went around in a golden haze, basking in her success. People noticed her more than previously. But the days went by, and the weeks. It was October; in the distance Mont St. Hilaire was a mass of yellow and brown and red against the clear blue sky. There were new entertainments—few plays, none with parts for Sheila—and other new events.

Dear Daddy, she wrote. *Here's the latest news at school. Sally's cat ran away last week and I was glad! I really hate that animal, he has such a mean face. But he came back yesterday, worse luck, and his ear is torn. Sally says this low stable life is ruining her baby. But I feel a lot more sorry for the other cat!*

Life is noisy these days because we hear a big CRASH every now and then. The new boy called Phil the Pill keeps breaking windows with wild kicks and throws of various balls. We're beginning to suspect he's doing it on purpose.

In English we are studying Hamlet, Prince of Denmark. *Hamlet seems like a very lonely person. But he sure talks a lot—*

"Hey, kids—" Mimi's voice interrupted the flow of Sheila's pen—"next week's Thanksgiving already! And the school orchestra is going to perform an original work by Tony."

"Oh, yes. It's a symphony," said Sally, "for piano, flute, violin, drums, dinner gongs, whistling kettles, vacuum cleaners, and typewriters. It sounds *wild*."

Sheila recounted this piece of news in her letter and added: *Now I understand why I've been hearing vacuum cleaners in the living room all the time lately. I thought the rug must be awfully dirty, but I guess they were just rehearsing.* She frowned a moment, then added: *I've read a lot of good books.* Too bad she had nothing more exciting to say about herself. She concluded, *Love, Sheila,* and then began a short, dutiful letter to Mother, who wrote her twice a week.

After Thanksgiving dinner, filled with turkey, the whole school went into the living room. The musicians grouped themselves around the piano, the typists seated at small tables. Tony, as conductor, looked darkly handsome in his best suit instead of his usual jeans. He bowed to the audience, turned to face the orchestra, raised his baton: and, with a loud roar from the Electrolux, the first movement began.

The second movement was slow and quiet: flute and typewriters, with crescendos underlined by the boiling of the electric kettles. This was the most difficult movement. It had taken a great deal of practice to time the kettles so they would whistle at the right moment. Tony, unlike Mimi, did not approve of improvisation in art. He had written a very exact score, inventing new musical notations for the less conventional instruments. The only member of the orchestra allowed freedom was the First Typist, Martha Duffield, who composed a piece of free verse.

The third movement was dazzling in its originality. Martha rose, removed the sheet of paper from her machine, and read

ED. NOTE: Canadian Thanksgiving is in October.

the poem aloud in a mysterious monotone, punctuated by dinner gongs.

During the fourth movement the ancient upright Hoover gave out, so the Electrolux had to do a solo. Throughout an almost deafening finale the piano tinkled sadly in the background.

There was a loud roar of applause and much laughter. Tony gave the audience a low, sweeping bow. His face was very solemn, but as he rose it suddenly burst into a delighted grin. Undoubtedly his symphony was the sensation of the term. They were still talking about it at the Sunday meeting three days later.

". . . though Tony's experimental stuff is awfully *gimmicky*," Janet was saying as Sheila entered the library. Janet felt disgruntled because so much of her flute playing had been drowned out by the Electrolux.

"I have a complaint to lodge against the Symphony," Rosalie put in. She sat curled prettily on the hearthrug. "Now we've got only one vacuum cleaner that works!"

"Oh, I've fixed the Hoover, Rosie," Willy assured her. Willy could fix anything.

"I've got another complaint," said Liz. "Please, whoever's been clogging up the cloakroom john with used carbon papers, stop it."

"What's that got to do with Tony's symphony?" asked Mike.

"I didn't say it had anything to do with Tony's symphony. I just said, *stop*."

"I've got a complaint too," Dick announced. "It's Ben. He's been disobeying the silence rule in the second-floor study all week, coming out with his maniac laugh and de*liberately* distracting everybody. It's so juvenile."

Ben looked embarrassed. "I won't do it again."

"Oh, yeah?"

"Maybe Ben should be made to laugh on the other side of his face," Willy suggested lightly. "I've always wondered about that expression. It sounds painful, doesn't it?"

"I know!" said Dick. "Ben, I think you should be made to sit in the study and laugh steadily for an hour."

"An *hour?*" Ben protested. "Come *on!*"

"An hour's too much," Tony decided. "Say, half an hour. He deserves that, but no more."

The proposal was carried by unanimous vote. Kenner students believed in letting the punishment fit the crime.

Sheila always went to the Sunday meetings because it meant being with other people. During the day she was so often alone.

"Given up speedball these days, Sheila?" Liz asked at lunch, the Monday after Thanksgiving.

"Well, yes."

"Maybe you'll enjoy winter sports more next term," Liz said kindly. She drained her water glass and stood up. "Well, see you at dinner!" Then she hurried away.

How *busy* they all were, Sheila thought. By the time she had finished her third helping of apple fritters, everyone else had left the dining room. Faintly, from outdoors, she could hear the sounds of a new speedball game. What energy these kids had! Especially the boys; they were tireless. She decided to go up to her room and read.

Passing the second-floor study, she heard cheerless, mechanical laughter coming through the door: "Ha, ha, ha, ha, ha, ha . . ." The voice paused wearily, and another voice broke in. "Don't stop now—still thirteen minutes to go." Poor Ben! He might not laugh again for weeks.

Neither Mimi nor Sally was in the bedroom. They hardly ever were. What were they doing? They didn't seem to have many courses. Sheila felt as lonely as she had the first morning of term. All the rest of the school seemed to have completely forgotten *Nothingness* and the green-faced girl. She was right back where she had started six long weeks ago.

And she was far lonelier than she had been at her last school. There she was always part of a group, sitting in a row of desks doing assignments or playing games in the gym. She hadn't liked it much, but she hadn't felt like an outcast, either. Now she spent so much time in this room, reading or daydreaming. Her daydreams were beginning to seem rather thin. She had a feeling that all kinds of exciting real-life things were going on around her, but she remained outside them.

She opened her new library book, *The Opium Den Mystery*, and was soon deeply absorbed in an exciting story. At six thirty Mimi and Sally came bursting into the room.

"Hi!" Sheila looked up, overjoyed to see them. Sally had a smear of paint on one cheek; Mimi's slacks were muddy. "What've you been doing?"

"Oh, nothing much," said Mimi. "Come on down to dinner— I'm *starving*."

After dinner there was always a group of kids in the library, toasting marshmallows or playing darts. And in the morning Sheila had English to look forward to. Rosalie's class was a lot of fun.

Sheila felt a certain sympathy for the hero of *Hamlet* right from the start. He too had a stepfather problem. Hamlet's father, the king of Denmark, had died recently; Hamlet's uncle was now king and had married Hamlet's widowed mother, Gertrude. The ghost of Hamlet's father appeared to him one night on the castle battlements and told Hamlet that his uncle had murdered his father for the throne of Denmark. Hamlet promised to avenge his father's death by killing his wicked uncle.

The main action of the play concerned the long time it took Hamlet to get around to doing this: his doubts, fears, anger, and reflections about life. To disguise his thoughts, he decided to pretend he was mad. The class had a long argument over whether Hamlet really did go mad or not.

"I don't think he's mad," said Tony. "In fact, I think he's the sanest person in the play. He understands more about life than the others do."

"But what about his manic-depressive tendencies?" Mike pointed out. "Look at the way he's so melancholy one moment and excited the next."

"Yes," said Jerry, "he has the classic symptoms. Still, I don't think he actually crosses the borderline into psychosis. He's just neurotic."

"Aren't we all!" said Tony, and everybody laughed.

Sheila didn't have the psychological sophistication to keep up with the discussion. The others talked about things like the "Oedipus complex"; she felt very naive. But Jerry, brought up by psychologists, was the star of the class.

At the end of the play Hamlet finally did kill his uncle. In fact, nearly everybody died, including Hamlet himself; Sheila could imagine the stage littered with dead bodies. Ophelia, Hamlet's sweetheart, went mad herself and drowned tragically because he no longer loved her.

"Hamlet certainly has a complex about women," Janet commented. "Look at how mean he is to his mother *and* his girl! I adore him, but all the same I hope I never fall in love with a man like him." Everybody laughed.

"I must say, I don't have much respect for Hamlet," said Dick. "He takes so long to make up his mind to kill Claudius; the play is interminable. Boy, if *I* were going to murder somebody, I wouldn't waste much time. As soon as I'd decided what method to use—poison or stabbing or whatever—I'd get going."

Rosalie smiled at this, then grew serious. "Dick, Hamlet can't kill his uncle right away because he's not yet *emotionally ready*. By the end he *is* emotionally ready; so then the actual act of murder is a simple matter."

Sheila said suddenly, "I feel sorry for Hamlet—he's so lonely. He has nobody who understands him, so he has to talk to himself all the time. He can't com*municate* with anybody; he's like the old man in the garbage pail in *Nothingness*. He isn't *in* a garbage pail—he moves around a lot—but he might just as well be."

"When are we going to start on *Finnegans Wake?*" Mimi put in quickly, anxious to change the subject. The performance of *Nothingness* was an event she didn't much like to remember.

Finnegans Wake, Sheila found, was a very long novel. When she opened the book at random, a sentence caught her eye:

> Well, arundgirond in a waveney lyne aringarouma she pattered and swung and sidled, dribbling her boulder through narrowa mosses, the dilisky-drear on our drier side and the vilde vetchvine agin us, curara here careero there, not knowing which medway or weser to strike it, edereider, making chattahoochee all to her ain chichiu, like Santa Claus at the cree of the pale and puny. . . .

What? But it was all like that: pages and pages. Rosalie said it was about a man sleeping and what went on in his subconscious. Well, Sheila had heard that the subconscious was a mysterious thing; this proved it. She couldn't make head or tail of it. Neither could the class.

"Now, don't be so *solemn* about *Finnegans Wake*," Rosalie urged them. "I know it's very obscure, but it's also funny."

"Funny!" said Mike. "It's not so funny when you're trying to plough your way through." (Not that he was trying very hard. He'd given up at page three.)

To show them what a funny book it was, Rosalie persuaded Willy to cancel his Contemporary Canadian Politics class one morning and visit the English room. One of Willy's many talents was an ability to imitate accents. He read several pages aloud in an authentic Irish brogue. It still didn't make much sense; yet somehow it *was* terribly funny, and the class decided they loved the book. Rosalie showed them how James Joyce made up new words; this inspired them to try and make some up themselves. For several days the English students went around saying things like "dragick" and "cuprical," which mystified everyone else.

After *Finnegans Wake* Ogden Nash's humorous verse was a refreshing contrast. Everyone's favorite (except Sally's) was very short:

> The trouble with a kitten is that,
> Eventually, it becomes a cat.

Sally didn't agree. "Cats are even nicer when they grow up," she insisted; but she liked Nash's other poems. The class read straight through his complete works, then wrote frivolous verse of their own. One of Sheila's went:

> The trouble with a kitten *or* a cat
> Is that
> Whenever one comes near me my eyes water and my
>   nose gets stuffed up and my throat gets hoarse
>   and I sneeze and sneeze and sneeze and sneeze—
>   AH-CHOO!—until I don't know where I'm
>   at.

Even Sally had to laugh when Rosalie read this aloud.

After English period Sheila would get another book from the

library and go back to her room. Mother had sent her Mexican rug, vase, and shell as requested; her side of the room looked attractive and personal now. But it stayed the same. She just put her things there and left them. Sally was always adding small decorative touches; Mimi continually rearranged her mice or made changes in the list of "Resolutions" pinned over her mirror:

1) Eat no sweet or greasy things for a whole year (except Christmas).

2) Learn to walk gracefully.

3) Get to know X.

4) Stop being afraid of spiders. It's neurotic.

5) Read Anna Karenina.

6) Read the Bible.

7) Stop growing!!!

"Who's X?" Sheila asked her one day.

Mimi blushed. "It's a secret."

"Oh, come on, Meem," said Sally, "everybody knows you have a crush on him."

"Sheila doesn't seem to. Why should I tell her?"

"Is it Jerry?" Sheila asked, rather hurt by this remark.

"Yes." Mimi sighed. "I just wish he'd *grow* a bit—just one inch!" Because he was an inch shorter, she went around with her shoulders slumped. It wasn't easy to slump and be graceful at the same time.

The new boy Jerry is terribly busy, Sheila wrote in one of her long letters to Daddy. *He's always rushing off to classes. He doesn't approve of coed sports and he argues a lot. I thought this would make the kids not like him, but he's POPULAR! He*

72

gets on with everybody, he has a good personality. Mimi says his smile is divine and the way his eyes twinkle. She says his eyes are a very special shade of blue-gray that she adores, but they look plain light blue to me. We call him the School Conservative.

Phil the Pill doesn't have any friends at all. I wonder if he's lonely, like Hamlet? Believe it or not, he isn't taking a single course! Sometimes I see him in the library, but he never talks to me. He chooses adventure books like Seven Years with the Amazon Head-Hunters. He plays speedball a lot.

"Phil's broken *eight* windows now!" Sheila told her roommates, looking up from her letter.

"Eight isn't much," said Sally scornfully. "When Ben was new last year he broke thirteen windows in one month. Definitely a school record," she said proudly.

"Oh, Ben was just a silly little kid then," Mimi exclaimed. "He was just showing off. When everyone got bored with his breakages, he got bored too. We seem to have a window breaker every year, Sheila—kind of a school tradition. Phil is different. He's *serious*."

Sheila added to her letter: *We seem to have a window breaker every year. It's kind of a school tradition.* She paused a moment, then wrote, *I still read a lot of books.*

"A lot of books have been mysteriously disappearing," Rachel, the library officer, declared at the next Sunday meeting. "Many of the titles listed aren't on the shelves *or* signed for. I've been trying to track down *The Opium Den Mystery* for *days*."

"Sheila's got it," said Sally. "There's a huge pile of books under her bed—she never brings them back."

"I do so!" said Sheila indignantly. "I just forget sometimes."

"Sheila, you *must* remember to sign for your books," said Rachel. "I'm afraid you'll have a huge overdue fine." She smiled at Sheila almost approvingly. Most people had been bringing their books back promptly, so the library fund hadn't made any money this term. With Sheila, Rachel had finally hit the jackpot.

"What about Phil?" Sheila was feeling disagreeable. "I often see him take out books without signing, and I bet he doesn't bring them back, either."

"If we asked him to, he'd probably dump them in the river instead," said Jerry.

They all agreed there was nothing they could do about Phil, who never came to the Sunday meetings. Some people just weren't community-minded.

As the term wore on, Sheila grew bored as well as lonely. Surely Kenny didn't *really* mean her to go on taking only English indefinitely?

"Hello, Kenny," Sheila greeted her rather shyly in the garden one day. "When am I going to start taking French and math and so on?" she asked uneasily.

"You've decided you want to take them?"

"Not really, but . . . I have so much free time."

"Well, then"—Kenny smiled warmly—"why not spend that time doing something you really *do* want to do?"

So Sheila read more books from the library.

Her birthday arrived: a rather soggy cake, baked by Madame; "Happy Birthday, dear Sheila"; and she was thirteen.

Phil broke six more windows.

Sally's cat ran away again.

Mimi grew half an inch.

And Rosalie gave an English test. Her pupils got the surprise of their lives when they entered the room to find it full of tables, and perched on the back of the sofa—a blackboard! Nobody had ever seen a blackboard at Kenner before. Rosalie sat below it, smiling rather wickedly. On the blackboard was written:

TEST

1) Is the ghost of Hamlet's father a real ghost or a figment of Hamlet's imagination?

2) What *happens* in *Finnegans Wake?*

3) Is Ogden Nash a true poet? Why? What *is* poetry? Quote freely.

4) *Very Important.* Write a detailed essay of everything you have been reading besides the class books. Did you enjoy them, or not? Why? Do you think they are good literature? Why? Please include *all* outside reading, including comic books. They have some value of their own.

5) Write an essay on "What Boarding School Has Done for Me." Has it done what you expected? What do you think a school should do for its students?

"Well, I'll leave you to it." She passed out paper and ball-point pens. "You can have all day, if you need it, with a break for lunch. Don't bother cheating; it can't help you answer these questions." She went away.

"What's got *into* her?" Mimi was bewildered. "We've always just *discussed* things before."

"I don't think the ghost is a real ghost, do you?" said Sally. "It's a hallucination in Hamlet's mind."

"It seems real to *me*," said Gaby. "It's so scary."

"I haven't *done* any outside reading," Jerry grumbled. "How could I? With so many courses, I haven't the time."

"Never mind that question, then," Pierre advised him. "You can have a lot of fun with question two."

"And question three," said Tony. "But let's all agree not to do question five. It's Rosie being nosy again."

"But there isn't anything *else* I can do," Mimi said plaintively. "I haven't read the Bible, I haven't read *Anna Karenina*,

I can't think how to answer the first three questions . . . Oh, Rosalie, what's *happened* to you?"

Sheila wasn't worried about question 4, anyway. If necessary she could write all day about the library books she had read.

On cold, dark mornings, rooms were awfully chilly, beds very comfortable. The bell was out of order again. It was very tempting, and easy, to murmur "I'm awake" to the knock on the door and go back to sleep.

"I don't feel emotionally ready for classes today," Mimi mumbled sleepily, one especially bleak morning late in November. "There's no point in me going—I wouldn't be an asset to the class and I wouldn't learn a thing."

"What's 'emotionally ready' mean?" Sheila asked curiously. She remembered having heard Rosalie use this expression.

"Oh, it means—it means—well, *you* know . . . um . . . emotionally *ready*. I mean, well, ready *emotionally*. . . ." Mimi gave up. "Can you explain it, Sal?"

"No," Sally replied. "But I'll tell you one thing: I'm not emotionally ready for a whole morning without food, are you? If we don't get up soon, breakfast will be gone."

So they got up. But that evening Mimi said, "I snitched some bread and cheese from the kitchen this aft, so if we don't feel emotionally ready for class tomorrow, we needn't go hungry."

The next morning they felt, if anything, even less emotionally ready for classes than the day before. They huddled cozily under blankets in the dimness of the room, curtains still drawn. They munched stale bread and cheese, talked lazily, and played a game with Mimi's mice. It was like a picnic.

"This is fun," said Sheila. "Let's be emotionally not ready for class more often."

"Mimi and I would get bored with nothing to do," said Sally.

Her tone implied that Sheila never had anything to do anyway.

"Gosh, yes," said Mimi. "When I first came to Kenner, I just loafed. In six weeks I was bored out of my *mind*."

"Mike lasted six *months*," Sally remembered. "He did nothing but play his banjo—till finally even he couldn't take it any longer." She frowned suddenly across the room. "Say . . ." She jumped up, shivering in the chilly air, hurried to the window, and pulled back the curtain. "Look! It's *snowing*."

Large soft flakes were falling swiftly; the ground was all covered with white. Several students were out in the garden throwing snowballs. "I bet all the rest are in back," said Mimi. "Gee, the whole school must be emotionally not ready for classes today!"

They quickly got into warm clothes and hurried outdoors.

Behind the building they found a wild snowball fight in progress. Others were trying out sleds and skis, but not skates; the ice on the river wasn't safe yet. Tony and Dick took Sally for a ride on their toboggan, and she squealed with excitement in the cold air. Mimi and Sheila were caught up in the snowball fight. Phil was the most energetic one, packing hard snowballs with a grim expression. Sheila bent down to get a handful of snow— Whack! Something hit her on the forehead. She came to a few seconds later and found herself lying in the snow, while faces peered down anxiously.

"You all right?" Jerry asked. His eyes were full of concern.

"I think so. Just a bit dizzy . . . and my head hurts."

"You're going to have a magnificent bruise on your left temple."

Jerry turned and glared up at Phil, who was standing by sullenly.

"Do you have to deliberately pack the snow as hard as a rock? She might have concussion."

"Oh, concussion's *terrible*," Mimi exclaimed. "My little sister fell off a horse once, and she's never been quite the same since. She gets headaches a lot." She looked down with a sympathetic concern Sheila didn't find very comforting.

"I didn't deliberately hit her," Phil insisted. "I aimed it at Jerry."

"Thanks a lot."

Sheila, sitting up, decided she felt better. Her head was clear now. But Jerry fussily insisted she must go indoors and rest in case of concussion. "Now, don't you dare stand up," he said sternly; "we'll carry you on Tony's toboggan." He wouldn't even let her sit on it; she had to lie back as though on a stretcher. Jerry and Tony pulled the toboggan up the hill, Mimi walking anxiously behind. Phil, scowling, made another tightly packed snowball. He flung it toward the building with great force—just as Kenny came out accompanied by a middle-aged couple. The snowball whizzed by, knocking the man's hat off his head—displacing a neat black hairpiece—then continued on: through the living room window—CRASH!—and across the long length of the room to the windows at the front—another CRASH!

Ben, standing at one side of the house, observed the whole thing. "Gee!" he said admiringly. "What a fantastic shot!"

Kenny and the strange couple stopped, startled; the man readjusted his toupee. They had seen Phil throw the snowball; but he didn't go up and apologize. He rejoined the snowball fight, which continued after a brief pause.

Jerry and Tony now came past the three adults, pulling Sheila, Mimi following behind.

"Hello, Kenny," said Mimi. "I'm afraid we can't wait to be introduced to your guests—we've got to get Sheila indoors quickly, in case she's got concussion."

"Concussion?" said the strange woman. The man said nothing; he was dusting snow off his hat with a frown.

"A snowball hit her on the head," Jerry explained. The three adults looked down at Sheila, who felt rather foolish. She closed her eyes and tried to look pathetic.

"Take her up to Mildred," Kenny said calmly. The ambulance crew hurried on indoors. Below, the snowball fight continued.

Chapter Seven

"*H*ey, kids—" Gaby burst breathlessly into the library that evening—"have you heard? That man and woman— you know, the bald one who at first wasn't—they're rich friends of the Kenners and they were considering donating money to the school so it won't have to close down next year and us switch to other schools . . ." She paused momentarily, for breath, then continued: "Mr. Bartell's a millionaire or something, and Mrs. B. is kind of interested in education; but after the snowball fight this morning, they were so mad they're not going to."

"Just because of that?" Mike exclaimed. He was standing at the other end of the room, feeding Louise. Flies being scarce in winter, she had to be content with dried fish food. "It was only Phil who did anything to them, and he just happens to be a nut."

"Well, but it seems that they're mad about everything. They don't approve of the whole school out snowball-fighting at eleven Tuesday morning instead of in class. Isn't it unfair? I mean, what do they expect, the first day of snow? It's mostly melted now. If we hadn't had our snowball fight this morning, we might have had to wait weeks till the next snowfall!"

There were murmurs of indignation all around the small group before the fire. Sheila, bruised but otherwise recovered, was toasting a marshmallow.

"If Mrs. Bartell is really *interested* in education," she remarked, "you'd think she might be more understanding about us not being emotionally ready for class the first day of snow."

"Oh, don't get hung up on that 'emotionally ready' expression for heaven's sake," Dick said scornfully. "We're free to go to class or not as we choose here; that's our privilege. So don't use silly, pompous words to describe something perfectly simple."

"But Mimi uses it a lot—"

"Oh, well, *Mimi* . . ."

"Mrs. Bartell told the Kenners we're not progressive at all," Gaby went on, impatient with the interruption. "She says we're *regressive* or something." Gaby was a valuable source of gossip. Her small size, soup-bowl haircut, and wide, innocent-looking dark-blue eyes seemed to be an asset when it came to overhearing things.

There were angry exclamations from the other six people present.

"And that's not all," she went on. "I just can't understand the Kenners—where's their pride? These people go and insult their school, and they're still polite to them! Believe it or not, the Bartells are coming over to have *tea* with Kenny and Willy tomorrow."

"I only wish *I* was making tea for them," Janet declared. "I'd see to it that a good dose of arsenic just happened to fall in the sugar."

The others took up her tune.

"Strychnine in the tea—"

"Deadly nightshade in the jam—"

"Something *really* awful in the applecake—"

"Well, why not?" Mike crossed the room, shaking his shaggy hair out of his eyes. "Not *poison*—we don't want to kill the

Kenners. But what about, say, just making the food kind of, well, revolting?"

"Yes!" Gaby's dark head bobbed up and down as she jumped excitedly. "Pepper in the jam. . . ."

"Salt in the sugar. . . ."

"Coffee in the tea—I tried it once. . . ."

"Mustard in the applecake. . . ."

"*Real* squashed flies in the squashed-fly biscuits. . . ."

"Ugh, Ben, what a revolting imagination!"

"No flies," said Gaby. "Flies are for Louise."

Janet looked more sober. "Who's going to do it? We can't *all* go; we'd be sure to get caught."

There was a long pause. Nobody was really very keen for the job. So they decided to draw lots. After a brief argument it was agreed that two should be drawn, to give each other moral support. Ben tore up a sheet of paper into seven scraps, made an X on two, and crumpled them up. Sheila unfolded hers apprehensively. Good! It was blank. . . .

"There's an X on the back of that, Sheila," Ben told her. Sheila's heart sank as she turned the scrap over; he was right. Gaby drew the other. She didn't mind so much.

"I think I can pick the lock on the kitchen door," Gaby said. "So if Madame locks it, we can still get in."

Sheila went to her room, three new library books under her arm: *A Tale of Two Cities, Wuthering Heights,* and *It's Like This, Cat.* She found Mimi and Sally crouched on the floor over a chessboard. Willy had been encouraging an interest in this game and gave lessons every Sunday. Already Sally wasn't too bad; at least she knew which way each piece was supposed to move. But Mimi was hopeless and moaned every time one of her pieces was captured. "Poor little thing," she mourned now as Sally took a pawn. "It's so small and helpless. I feel like such a worm for not defending it properly." She looked up. "Hi, Sheil. How's Louise? I haven't visited her today."

"Rather droopy. I don't think she likes fish food—it lacks vitamins or something." Sheila looked down at them thoughtfully. They didn't know about the revenge plot yet. The conspirators had decided to keep their plans quiet until completed, in case word spread too far. But Mimi and Sally could be trusted with a secret. However, all of a sudden Sheila decided she wasn't going to tell them. They were involved in so many things that didn't include her; she deserved to have a secret from them. She'd tell them afterward and they would all laugh together.

The conspirators planned thoroughly. At three o'clock Madame went out to visit her grandchildren, locking the kitchen and taking her keys with her. She left the food ready for the tea party on a tray; all Kenny would have to do when the Bartells arrived was boil a kettle and fill the teapot. The Kenners would both be busy till three-thirty—Willy in the carpentry workshop, Kenny in the biology lab. The guests were expected at four.

At ten past three, seeing the coast clear in the dining room, Sheila and Gaby approached the kitchen door in stocking feet. Gaby had stolen a Squash Club membership card from Willy's desk drawer. "These stiff shiny cards are just the thing for picking a certain standard kind of lock," she told Sheila. Luckily the kitchen lock *was* this kind. Gaby slid the card in the door crack, pushed the latch back (a talent for which she was noted), and they went inside.

They found a plate of jam tarts, a bowl of sugar, a jug of milk, a pot of tea with tea leaves in the bottom, and a large chocolate layer cake.

"Chocolate cake!" Gaby exclaimed indignantly. "I see she's not serving *them* apples!"

Pepper, sprinkled in the jam and stirred thoroughly, blended easily with the red color. Salt in the sugar bowl was even easier. Coffee and pepper mixed inconspicuously with the tea leaves at the bottom of the pot. The cake was more of a problem. How to spoil it without changing its outward appearance?

"Let's not bother," Sheila urged, nervously glancing at her watch.

But Gaby was determined. So they carefully removed the top layer with a wide spatula, scooped out most of the inside of the bottom—which they ate—and filled the hole with a mixture of mustard, coffee, salt, pepper, paprika, and oregano. Sheila added a dollop of dog food for good measure. They carefully replaced the top layer and smoothed the thick icing over the join. "The top's still edible, of course," Gaby mourned, "but maybe the bottom will put them off enough so they'll lose their appetite. Mustard and chocolate! Ugh, just mustard alone makes *me* sick."

Deciding not to bother about the milk, they left the room. Gaby looked back before closing the door. "Doesn't it all look delicious?" she whispered gleefully. "Who would ever *dream!*"

At four o'clock Mike, doing reconnaissance work outdoors, saw the Bartells' black Cadillac arrive. At half past five the Bartells came out of the house, bidding friendly farewells to the Kenners at the door. Mike heard the two of them chuckling faintly as they got into their car. He had an uncomfortable feeling that the revenge hadn't been too impressive.

At dinner the conspirators were tense with expectation. But the Kenners behaved perfectly normally. No word was mentioned about the afternoon's tea, not by anybody. Sheila and Gaby might very well never have doctored the food at all.

After dinner, before leaving the room, Kenny paused in the doorway. Her tone was superbly casual.

"Willy and I would be pleased to have Sheila and Gaby for coffee with us in the study."

Then she was gone. Sheila and Gaby stiffened. It was a common custom for the Kenners to invite small groups of students, sometimes the other teachers as well, for coffee and dessert after dinner. Adults and children would discuss school affairs, tell jokes, and listen to Willy's jazz records. But why only the two of them, on this particular evening? Both of them knew why. It couldn't be a coincidence.

Sheila and Gaby lingered over the remains of their meal until after all the others had left—without appetite, putting off the inevitable.

"Well," Sheila said finally, "guess we'd better go."

"Let's not. Why should we? We don't have to go to classes when we don't feel like it. Why should we go to coffee? I hate coffee anyway."

A sudden dark suspicion entered Sheila's mind.

"I bet it's not coffee. I bet it's tea. *Cold* tea."

Gaby turned pale.

"Sheila—no! They wouldn't!"

"Oh, wouldn't they?"

"Then I'm not going!"

"But, Gaby," Sheila said nervously, "you can't just ig*nore* the invitation. . . ."

"Why not?"

"Maybe they won't really give us that revolting food. Maybe they'll just lecture us and make us feel like worms."

"But the Kenners don't *do* that," Gaby said irritably. "We all vote on what anybody's punishment should be. . . ."

Willy appeared in the doorway. "What's the delay, girls? Come on, or the coffee will be cold."

Coffee? The word filled them with fresh hope. They followed

him into the study, where Kenny was indeed pouring out coffee. She smiled at them. *"Café au lait,* girls?"

"Oh, I like mine black," Gaby said hastily. Not that the milk had been doctored, only the sugar; but it couldn't hurt to be on the safe side. The coffee itself must be all right, since the Kenners were drinking it.

"A sophisticated taste," Willy remarked pleasantly. "Sugar?"

"No, thanks. I *never* take sugar, it's bad for the teeth."

Sheila frowned; Gaby was overdoing it.

"Well, I know *Sheila* takes sugar." Before she could stop him, he had put two large spoonfuls in her cup. Sheila sipped it gingerly. To her amazement, it tasted all right. She gave a little smile of triumph to Gaby, who, stuck with a cup of bitter black coffee, scowled back.

"Now I've got a special treat for you two," said Kenny, and their hearts sank. "Raspberry jam tarts and a delicious chocolate layer cake. Willy and I won't eat any, as we have to watch our figures."

The sight of the cake was too much for Gaby.

"It's not fair! There were seven of us in the plot—we drew lots; Sheila and I got the job. You can't make me eat it! I absolutely re*fuse."* She held her hands behind her back and would not accept the plate which Kenny offered her.

"What about you, Sheila?" Kenny asked gently.

Sheila admired Gaby's firmness; she didn't feel so bold herself. Uneasily she eyed the cake. It looked even more revolting than she remembered. Kenny had cut two slices, and the dog food was visible. Sheila could even smell it.

"It looks delicious," she said finally. "But, well, maybe a bit too *rich."*

Suddenly Willy laughed. Kenny put down the cake and tarts on the coffee table, and everyone laughed merrily. The two girls smiled at each other in joyful relief. They weren't going to have to eat the stuff after all.

"How did you know it was Sheila and me?" Gaby asked cheerfully.

"Mildred reported seeing you coming away from the kitchen this afternoon, very stealthily."

"Oh! We never noticed her. What did the Bartells think of their tea?"

"They were very nice about it," said Willy. "They even laughed. But, girls, you *did* ruin our food. We can't just ignore that. So we'll bring up the matter at the next Sunday meeting."

"Then everybody can decide whether you should be punished, and how," Kenny added, "in the usual way."

So they weren't going to get away with it after all. Sheila had an unpleasant conviction that a majority of students would vote in favor of eating the food as punishment. It fit the crime so perfectly. Meeting Gaby's eyes, she knew her partner in crime was thinking the same thing.

"It wasn't just us," Gaby protested. "Ben and Janet and Mike and—"

"Never mind that now," said Willy. "You can discuss it on Sunday."

Sheila looked at the cake again, and her courage dimmed. The tarts didn't look quite so bad. With sudden resolution, she snatched one off the plate and dramatically pushed it into her mouth whole. She choked, coughed, gagged, spluttered, and finally got it down with the help of her coffee. "Whew!" She wiped her eyes and smiled weakly.

Kenny and Willy grinned back. Gaby, not to be outdone by Sheila, grimly took a tart from the plate. She struggled through it, then wiped her mouth, with a deep, gloomy sigh.

"Nice and spicy, aren't they?" said Kenny. "Now, how about some cake?"

Gaby burst into tears.

"I won't—I won't—you can't make me! I never *can* eat mustard, not even on hot dogs—it makes me sick! I just *won't!*"

"I think that'll be enough, girls," said Willy nervously. Sheila decided he was afraid they really would be sick. The relief made her suddenly very composed.

"Thanks so much for the delicious dessert," she said, rising. Gaby said nothing; she wasn't feeling too well.

"You're welcome, girls," said Kenny graciously. "I'll tell Madame how much you praised her cooking."

Sheila hurried up to the library—without Gaby, who had gone off to lie down. She found her fellow conspirators before the fire, plus Mimi and Sally. Janet looked up eagerly. "Sheila! What happened?"

"Oh, just the usual *café au lait*," said Sheila airily. "And a really *yummy* dessert—pepper tarts and mustard cake."

"Oh, gee, Sheil, I'm sorry you two had to get all the blame!" But Janet looked more relieved than sorry. "How much did you have to eat?"

"Well, just a tart—but that was *quite* enough, thanks! I'd like to see *you* munch your way through one. . . ." Sheila noticed that Mimi and Sally were eyeing her coldly. Why Mimi? What was wrong? She had expected interest and sympathy from Mimi —or at least laughter.

"You deserved to eat *all* the stuff," Mimi burst out abruptly. "What a silly, corny, infantile revenge! It's—it was so *square.*" The word was loaded with scorn.

"But, Mimi"—Sheila stared at her in dismay—"Seven of us plotted it. And it was Janet's idea in the first place—"

"It was *not,*" Janet protested. "It was Mike's idea."

"Oh, I don't care whose idea it was," Mimi declared. "Sheila and Gaby were the ones who did it."

"But we *all* drew lots," Janet said, anxious to be fair.

"I don't care. Sheila and Gaby *did* it. Gaby's just a silly little kid, but Sheila's old enough to know better. It was so *corny*."

Sheila was suddenly furious. "Oh, I'm so *sick* of you all," she burst out. "You're all so darn selfish, going around being individuals all the time. You don't care about anything but yourself."

"Oh, we don't?" Mimi's face was red with anger. "And what about *you*, always moping around feeling so sorry for yourself? I suppose you call that *un*selfish?"

"Oh, shut *up!*"

"I will *not* shut up!"

"Yes, you *will!* Shut *up*—"

"I will *not* shut up so long as you keep yelling at me and telling me I'm selfish. I've been darn nice to you; I gave you the lead in my play—"

"It *wasn't* the lead! It was just a stupid little part, and I *made* it good."

"Well, that's the last part you'll get in any play of *mine*—"

"That's the last part I *want* in any play of yours, thanks."

Sheila was fearful that if the argument went on much longer, Mimi might have the last word. It was definitely time to make an exit while the going was good.

"And I've had just about enough of this ridiculous, infantile argument," she declared, eyes blazing, then turned and marched from the room. The loud slam she gave the door was very satisfying.

She seethed with anger all the way down to her room: anger and hate. I hate Mimi, hate Sally, hate Mimi; I hate them all. . . . But suddenly the anger left her, and she collapsed into tears on her bed. Now everything was ruined. She had lost Mimi's friendship; and Mimi was the only friend she had in the school. She had lost every bit of prestige she had gained as the green-faced girl. She had hit rock bottom; she might as well give up. She would write Mother and ask if she could leave.

But she didn't. She finally got up and went to the bathroom to soak in a warm tub. She passed Rosalie in the corridor; the teacher smiled at her. "Have a nice time with the Kenners, Sheila?" Sheila glared at her and hurried away. Rosalie obviously knew just what sort of a time it had been.

Mike told the story to his dormitory mates as they got ready for bed. They were less scornful than Mimi had been. They even laughed.

"You were lucky," Jerry pointed out. "You had all the fun of planning it without the danger."

"I know—those poor girls!" Mike didn't sound very sympathetic. Under its shaggy forelock, his round, snub-nosed face was amused. "Say, where's Phil? Gone for a little canoe trip?"

"Oh, Mike, aren't you sick of that old joke?"

"Sure. I'm sorry," said Mike, more bored than apologetic. Although nobody tried to make friends with Phil anymore—previous attempts having failed so dismally—they didn't bait him either. They let him alone. They were used to Phil now; in his own way, he belonged.

"I guess he's in the shower," said Don.

Pierre came in, cheerfully flushed after an energetic action-painting session in the art studio. He was wearing his artist uniform, an old trench coat smeared with all the colors of the rainbow.

"Talking about Phil *again?*" he said. "Oh! I overheard a remark Rosalie made to Mildred this morning—something about Phil being expelled from a military school before he came here."

"A military school!" Ian exclaimed. "Poor guy—no wonder he's neurotic."

"I wonder if his parents are divorced?" Jerry mused aloud.

"They're not."

"Oh." He frowned, then brightened suddenly. "Gee, that's even *worse!* When two neurotic parents stick together, it can make the child even more mixed up than if they get a divorce."

"Oh, don't be so smug," Don said irritably. "Just because *both* your parents are psychologists, you think you know everything."

"I guess the whole family needs an analyst," said Mike wearily. "The trouble is, I can't make myself feel sorry for Phil. He's so obnoxious."

"Shh," said Pierre. "Here he comes."

They all fell silent as Phil entered the room, wearing a handsome blue dressing gown. He frowned suspiciously, as though sensing that they had been talking about him.

"Hi, Phil," said Jerry amiably. "Say, did you hear what happened to Sheila and Gaby?"

"No."

His expression was not encouraging, but Jerry told the story anyway. Phil listened with interest, and at one point almost smiled. But when Jerry had finished, he said only, "Silly kids," his pinched features again unfriendly.

"Hey, boys"—it was Patrick, the bedtime officer, out in the hall—"if you don't get to bed in *ten minutes flat* . . ."

When the lights were out, there was the usual creaking of springs, whispers, and muffled laughs as everyone settled down. But Phil was silent. Peering at his tightly curled shape across the room, faintly lit by moonlight through the high windows,

Jerry wondered how he could ever fall asleep, he looked so tense. But in the morning he would be sprawled on his stomach, limbs flung out, blankets tangled, as though sleep left him exhausted instead of giving him rest.

Chapter Eight

*S*heila expected Mimi to be as cold to her as Sally was after that. To her surprise, the next day Mimi acted the same as ever, as though the fierce little squabble had never taken place at all.

Sheila and Gaby had to endure a lot of teasing from the rest of the school, both students and staff. "Pass the mustard, Gaby—but *don't* put it in the cake"; "Hey, Sheila, this stew looks a bit funny—sure you didn't add a little dog food to spice it up?" Gaby enjoyed her reputation, giggled, and made jokes about it herself. But Sheila felt a little silly.

The Christmas holidays drew near. Mimi and Sally looked forward to them eagerly, Sheila with mixed feelings. It would be a relief to get away from school for a while, to have her own room. Still, she wasn't sure how she would get on with Mother and Stan. It seemed a long time since that farewell on the train. But it was only three months!

"We're going up north skiing for Christmas," Mimi said excitedly. "I can't *wait!* It's funny—I always love coming to school, and then by the end of the term I can hardly wait to go home." She looked across the room at Sheila, who was sitting dreamily on the edge of her bed, gazing at nothing. "Aren't you excited, Sheila? It's your first boarding school holiday."

"I guess so," Sheila replied absently.

"What d'you mean, you *guess* so?"

Sheila decided it was high time Mimi and Sally realized everybody wasn't as lucky and well adjusted as themselves.

"Well, things are a bit difficult in my family, you know," she said, in a tone which suggested mature, world-weary patience with ignorant youth. "When two parents break up, the child is emotionally torn. And when the one he or she lives with re-marries, this just adds to the child's emotional burden." (She was quoting from the book Rosalie had given her—rather well, she felt.) "There's not only my uncertain attitude to Stan, as a stranger who's taken the place of my father; there's also his attitude to me, as a strange child he wouldn't choose to have if he hadn't married Mother. I just come along with her; it's a package deal." (She felt proud of this touch.) "Then, of course, there's Mother's situation. She feels guilty because, when she married him, she was more concerned with her own feelings than mine—she was being a *woman,* rather than a *mother.*"

She swung her foot with elaborate casualness, feeling she had expressed this rather brilliantly. Sally seemed impressed by her new psychological sophistication. But not Mimi.

"So what, for heaven's sake? Why *shouldn't* your mother consider her own feelings, anyway? Heavens, my parents are divorced too—you know that—but I don't go around feeling emotionally burdened all the time because of it."

"You don't have a stepfather," Sheila pointed out defensively.

"No, worse luck. I wish I *did.* It's high time Mum remarried—she needs a man. And she's so pretty, she deserves one."

Sheila had no answer to that.

"Now, I wonder . . ." Mimi was suddenly reflective. "If we could get your father and my mother together, maybe they'd hit it off. They'd make a divinely attractive mature couple."

"Daddy doesn't want to marry again," Sheila said jealously.

"He will. Everybody who's divorced gets remarried at least once. Still, I'm not so sure I'd want you as a stepsister."

"Nor me *you*," snapped Sheila, to be even.

The last day of school arrived. They would catch a train to Montreal that afternoon. On her way to the English classroom after breakfast, Mimi said suddenly, "I wonder if Rosalie will give us our papers back today?"

"What papers?" Tony asked absently.

"The test papers. It's over a month since we wrote them."

"Oh, that! Who cares? It was strictly for laughs, Mimi."

"Maybe she'll just give us a list of marks," Sheila suggested.

"*Marks?*" said Mimi scornfully. "We never have *marks*."

Rosalie smiled cheerfully when they all trooped into the room.

"As it's the last day of term, I thought it'd be fun to do something different—a debate. The topic is '*Resolved*, that boys are better than girls.'"

"But they're not," objected Gaby.

"Oh, you'll take the negative, of course. The boys will take the affirmative."

"What's affirmative?"

"The boys will try to show, through reasoned argument, that boys are better than girls. You girls will argue that boys are *not* better than girls."

"Can we argue that girls are better than boys?" Janet asked.

Rosalie looked at her with interest. "So you think girls are better than boys, Janet?"

"No, I just wanted to get the rules of the debate clear in my mind."

"You can argue whatever you like. Let yourself go."

"How *can* I argue that boys are better than girls?" Ben objected. "I don't think they are. Not much, anyway."

"Well, just for the sake of the debate, try to do your best to prove that boys are better than girls. It's all in fun."

But they didn't find it much fun. They were vaguely irritated by being asked to argue over such a corny subject. It was more than corny; it was boring. Mimi, however, anxious to impress Rosalie, spoke up at once.

"In the age we live in," she began earnestly, "I think being a girl is more re*warding*. I mean, look at all the things we can be. We can be independent career women, or mothers, or anything. We can wear slacks or frilly dresses. Gee, it's ex*citing* to be a girl nowadays! We can be *anything*. I feel kind of sorry for boys."

Jerry thought the debate childish and beneath his dignity; but, all the same, he couldn't let that remark pass.

"I guess you have a point there, Mimi, but all the same . . . thank goodness I'm a boy!" There were several chuckles as he said this. He spoke lightly; but suddenly, having said the words, he *did* feel grateful. Grateful to fate, or whatever it was, which had caused him to be born a boy, not a girl. What a wonderful piece of luck!

"How do you feel, Sheila?" Rosalie asked curiously.

"Oh . . . I don't know . . ." Sheila couldn't remember ever having thought about it. She hadn't ever wished she were a boy; but neither had she ever rejoiced at being a girl. She simply accepted it; she couldn't imagine being otherwise. "I guess I just am a girl," she said finally. "There's nothing I can do about it."

Everybody laughed at this. But then the debate flagged. Nobody really cared much whether boys were better than girls. Mike's insistence on men's superior energy received only half-hearted support from the other boys, although Jerry, as the school conservative, felt morally obligated to back him up. Janet's point that girls were more creative because they could have babies was regarded even by the girls as strictly square. They were all glad when Rosalie dismissed the class.

But when they went out the door, Mimi hung back.

"Please, Rosalie—what about the test?"

Rosalie was powdering her nose, looking in a compact mirror. "The test?"

"Yes . . . you know, that test you gave us."

"Ah, yes—the test." Rosalie took out a lipstick and painted her lips with frowning concentration.

"Well, what about it, Rosalie? I mean—what were our papers like?"

The teacher clicked her compact shut. She looked up with one of her sudden flashing smiles, then frowned solemnly. "Oh, very interesting, Mimi. Very interesting indeed." She took an address book from her pocket and studied it. Mimi felt dismissed.

"I just don't know what's got *into* her this term," she complained to Sheila. "She's acting so strange." She shook her head in bewilderment. " 'Boys are better than girls!' What *next!*"

Jerry, entering the dining room for lunch, smiled at everyone with more than his usual charm and good humor. The mealtime chatter was full of holiday excitement. A group at one table sang Christmas carols between mouthfuls of food.

The past week had been a lot of fun, now that the ice on the river was safe for skating. Next term they would get up a couple of hockey teams. By now he was almost resigned to having girls on them.

His studies weren't going too badly, either. He found not

only English but all his classes livelier than at his previous school. His classmates were less reserved, more likely to ask curious questions. The teaching was far better than he had expected. Willy's European history class was the most fun, though it also involved the most work: historical novels, biographies and autobiographies of famous people, besides straight history books. Sometimes they watched a historical film.

Kenny and Jeanne Dupont taught in a more conventional way than Willy or Rosalie. Standing before the chemistry and mathematics classes, Kenny's sparkling dark eyes, her wiry little body, her deep warm voice, were arresting; she fired the students with some of her enthusiasm for these subjects. Jeanne's class read many French-Canadian books and discussed them in French. Jerry had had a hard time keeping up with the conversations at first, but now he was beginning to speak the language more easily, with a distinct Canadian accent.

Yes, the school wasn't turning out too badly. Most surprising (for Jerry had at first regretted his rash decision to take it), his Latin lessons with Willy were a lot of fun. Willy's Latin was rusty, so they were learning together. Sometimes they played chess instead.

All the same, Jerry was happy to be going home for three weeks.

"Hi, Jerry!" It was Liz. For once she was wearing a dress instead of the usual baggy sweater and tight slacks favored by Kenner girls. "Guess we'll have some good hockey games next term, eh?"

Jerry frowned. He couldn't understand Liz's popularity. She was a keen leader, sure, and liked having people to lead. Okay, fine; but why did the other kids let her throw her weight around? They seemed positively to *like* her.

But suddenly he smiled, again filled with a rush of holiday spirit. "Guess so! See you next year, Lizzie."

She smiled festively and went off to a table. Jerry saw Phil serving himself at the sideboard. He went straight up to him.

"Next term we can play hockey, Phil," he said breezily with his most winning smile. "And I hear there's a good ski hill on Mont St. Hilaire."

Phil stared at him for a moment, then down at the floor. His mouth tightened. His whole body grew tense. His hands clenched into fists. Slowly he raised them, reached for the bowl of apples on the table, and exclaimed: "Oh, I just can't *stand* it!"

He flung the bowl on the floor with great force. It shattered, and apples went rolling all over the room. Then he marched out, tripped over an apple, fell, got up, and hurried on. Through the window Jerry saw him outside, in front of the house, hurrying toward the road. Then he was gone.

Everyone was frozen for a minute, stunned. Kenny stood clutching at the back of a chair as though for support. Everyone looked at her in surprise—especially Tony, who had been at the school for six years. Never before had he seen Kenny at a loss. Seeing her like this was more of a shock than Phil's outburst.

"I'll go after him, Bianca," said Willy quietly. It was the first time anyone had heard him call her "Bianca."

Willy left the room, and Kenny quickly regained her composure. "Will somebody please pick up these apples?" She turned and went out. A moment later Jerry saw Willy on the driveway, walking rapidly toward the road.

The holiday mood was broken. Mimi was feeling a little guilty over the nickname she had started: Phil the Pill. Jerry felt even more guilty. Phil had been his dorm mate all term, yet he had never felt any sympathy for him until now. Now, for the first time, he had gotten a glimpse of real unhappiness.

Willy soon returned, alone. He got out his old Ford, then started off again to search for Phil. The other students were bringing their suitcases downstairs to be loaded on the bus for the trip to the railway station. Jerry had just added his to the pile in the front hall when the door opened. Sally burst in, weeping.

"Help! The stable's on fire! Oh, help, help, help! Quick! I went out there to see if I could find Cat—and it's burning! If he *is* in there, he'll burn to death!"

The nearest fire department was called, and everybody hurried outside. Smoke was pouring out the stable door. "Quick!" Liz cried in panic. "If it spreads to the chem lab, something will blow up! The firemen won't get here in time!"

Dick and Tony plunged bravely into the smoke. Luckily the fire hadn't spread quite as far as the chemistry lab yet, though flames were moving near the open door. Some boxes of old books and magazines were blazing brightly. Dick pulled the fire extinguisher off the wall and quickly quenched the flames.

"Good going, Dick!" said Janet. "What started it?"

"Dunno. . . ." Dick wiped his smoke-stained, sweating face with the back of his hand. "Just these boxes were burning. Funny . . ."

"Look!" Tony bent down and saw several blackened matchsticks scattered over the floor. "No sign of a cigarette butt or anything," he observed. "Eleven . . . no, twelve matches, right where the fire started. . . . It's almost as though somebody had set fire to these boxes deliberately."

"Phil!" Dick exclaimed.

"Now, that's an unfair accusation. We've no evidence it was he."

"Oh, yeah? Who else?"

"How could he?" Jerry objected. "I saw him go straight to the road. He didn't go into the stable at all."

"He started the fire before lunch, then. He must have. Doesn't make much sense as an accident. All these matches!"

"But it *might* have been an accident, somehow. . . . Anyway, how can you be sure these matches started the fire? Somebody may've just dropped them." Jerry spoke halfheartedly. He had a strong conviction that Phil *had* deliberately set fire to the boxes. Several students went into the building to search, just in case Phil was hanging around.

Sally came out, still crying. "He's not here. Every day I put out food for him and call him, but he doesn't come. He's been gone a month now."

Just then a fire engine turned awkwardly into the drive.

"Oh, Sal"—Mimi tried to comfort her—"you know how wild he was getting. He's probably better off on his own."

"He doesn't love me anymore," Sally sobbed.

"Well, he never did really, did he? He was as vicious to you as anybody."

Kenny was having some difficulty in persuading the firemen to go away. They seemed to think they had been called by one of the students as a joke and inspected the small damage with suspicious looks.

"He respected me," Sally wept. "But now he's forgotten all about me. I'll never see him again. And it's all because of Sheila's silly psychosomatic allergy!"

The firemen finally went away. There was no sign of Phil in the stable; but Kenny continued to stand in the drive, anxiously waiting for Willy. The students began to grow restless. Until Willy returned there was nobody to drive them to the station. Nobody else had ever driven a bus and certainly didn't want to try on the icy winter roads. The students were worried about Phil, but also about missing their train.

Jerry sat in the living room, gazing out at the wintry outdoors. If he were Phil, what would he do? Where would he go? He tried to imagine how he'd feel if he started a fire (just supposing, for the moment, that Phil really *had*) and ran away in panic. Would he walk on the road? Not likely; he'd expect Willy to search for him in the car. He'd want to hide probably, but where? Somewhere off the road—across the fields, maybe. . . .

Suddenly Jerry jumped up. He dashed to the front hall, searched among the jumbled mass of overshoes for his own, and pulled them on. "Back soon," he said and hurried outdoors. The air was bitingly cold. The St. Jean farm—owned by Madame's son—was about a quarter of a mile down the road; it supplied the school with milk, butter, eggs, and apples. In one of the farther fields, Jerry knew, was a deserted barn; he'd seen it once from the bus on a trip to the village. Phil knew about it too. It seemed the best nearby hiding place for a frightened runaway.

It wasn't far, but trudging across the fields in knee-deep snow seemed interminable. Approaching the old weather-worn gray barn, Jerry slowed down, breathing heavily. Now he had come so far, he wondered why he had bothered. He could hardly drag Phil back by force—and anyway he wouldn't want to.

Across the fields Mont St. Hilaire rose up, a black-and-white patchy mass of snow and bare trees against the white winter sky. There would be more snow tonight. Jerry stopped outside the barn, feeling rather foolish. Phil probably wouldn't be there after all, and he'd have hurried all the way here for nothing.

Only half the old double door remained, hanging on its hinges. Jerry slowly and cautiously looked inside. The first thing he saw was a large tabby cat perched on an ancient crate. It looked at him with familiar crossed eyes. Entering, Jerry met the eyes of Phil, who sat in a corner wrapped in a moth-eaten old horse blanket, hugging himself to keep warm. Both he and the cat looked wild and wary.

"Hello," said Jerry gently, as he might speak to some nervous animal, afraid of scaring it away.

"Where's Mrs. Kenner?" Phil asked suspiciously.

"At school, of course."

"Where's Mr. Kenner?"

"Out looking for you with the car."

"Who came with you?"

"Nobody."

"You came alone?"

"Yes."

"Think you're going to drag me back or something?"

"I wouldn't dream of trying. Anyway, even if I could, what would be the point? You'd just run away again if you felt like it."

"Why did you come, then?"

Jerry shrugged his shoulders helplessly. "I really don't know."

"How did you track me down here?"

"Oh—just an inspiration."

Phil hugged himself sullenly. The cat lashed its tail. All three were silent for a moment. Then Jerry said, "Well, there's no point me hanging around. Bye," and started to go.

"You're going to tell them to come and find me. What's the point? By the time they get here, I'll be gone."

Jerry stopped in the doorway. "Look, I won't tell anybody you're here if you don't want me to."

"Oh, yeah. I'll *bet*."

"No, really. I won't tell anybody if you ask me not to. I promise." He was very anxious that Phil should believe him.

Phil was silent.

"You'd better make up your mind now," Jerry said. "I can't

wait much longer or I'll miss my train. Tell me if you want to keep this a secret."

"Oh, what's the point," Phil muttered wearily. "Go ahead and tell them I'm here. I won't go away. Tell them they can come and get me anytime. The sooner the better, really—it's so cold."

"You don't want to come back with me? Walking's warmer."

"No. They'll have to come and get me."

"All right." Jerry hesitated a moment, not happy about leaving so abruptly. "Do you really hate the school?"

"No more than other schools. I've been expelled from five—the last was a military school. They all said I was incurably antisocial. My parents persuaded the Kenners to give me a chance here, but of course I'm a hopeless case." He said this with a certain bitter pride.

Jerry felt horribly helpless and stupid. Of course he'd known other kids who were mixed up and unhappy, but nobody as bad as Phil. There was absolutely nothing he could do or say to help this angry, hate-filled boy.

"*Did* you set fire to the stable?" he asked hesitantly, in sudden hope that Phil hadn't.

"Of course I did," Phil snapped back.

"Oh. I saw you pass the stable and—"

"I slipped around to the back door."

"Oh."

Jerry stood there for a moment. "Good-by, Phil," he said sadly. He looked uncertainly at the cat, knowing Sally was worried about him. "Here, puss, puss, puss." The cat just lashed its tail. So Jerry went out.

When he arrived back at school, he went straight to Kenny and said, "I've found Phil and Sally's cat. They're in the deserted barn at the St. Jean farm. Phil says he'll stay there if you come and get him; I don't know about the cat. Phil admits he set fire to the stable."

The students didn't see Phil again. Kenny met him at the old barn and drove him into Montreal herself.

Willy got the others to the station well in time for the train. Kenny, before leaving for Montreal with Phil, had delivered Sally's cat at the school. He was now in his plaid bag, deeply drugged; and Sally was happy again.

"I want to thank you for finding Phil," Willy told Jerry while they waited for the train. The two had walked a little away from the others to talk privately. "I feel very bad about him. He's the only student we've had who finally became too much for the school to handle."

"I hear he's been expelled from other schools," Jerry said.

"Yes, but he wasn't so destructive there, more sullen and uncooperative. Being so free here made him start to become violent. We've had a few other kids at Kenner who were helped by being allowed to be destructive; they got it out of their systems and got bored with it. But none went so far as to deliberately start a fire. Broken windows we're used to; fires are just too dangerous. We simply can't afford to let him stay on."

"Why haven't his parents sent him to a psychiatrist?"

"I hope they will now. His father's terrified at the thought that his son is mentally sick. Tried to fool himself that discipline would do the trick, so he sent him to a military school—the worst possible place for a boy like Phil! Sending him here was a desperate last resort. His starting the fire should convince his parents that he needs psychiatric help."

"Phil thinks he's incurable." Jerry was still in a somber mood after the encounter in the barn. The other children's bright holiday chatter couldn't infect him. Sally was singing "O Little

Town of Bethlehem" in her sweet, pure voice, while Tony hummed a harmony. The familiar tune sounded terribly sad.

"Nonsense, of course he's curable. I only wish we could give him another chance at Kenner! But Kenny feels it's too risky, and I guess she's right. We have to think of the good of the whole school. Starting fires is just too dangerous." Willy sighed. "Here comes your train now. Have a nice holiday, Jerry. We'll play more chess next year."

Sheila's reunion with her mother and Stan was a joyful one. Mother was very happy to see her; even Stan seemed pleased. The first few days were full of shopping and merriment. Mother brought her breakfast in bed; she felt deliciously spoiled. For Christmas, Stan gave her a glossy new muskrat coat. "A fur coat for *me?*" Sheila exclaimed, stroking it unbelievingly. "A fur coat for *me!*" It far outshone the amber beads Daddy sent from Vancouver.

In spite of the coat, she and Stan got on less well as the holidays continued. They argued over silly little things. Stan would hardly speak to her for a long while, then he might say brusquely, "Sheila, take your feet off the sofa; your shoes are dirty." And Sheila would rebel.

"What right have you to order me around?" Her eyes blazed. "You're not my father." Then she would relapse into a brooding silence, her face sullen, her dark eyes unfriendly.

Stan would be silent, and she would know he was hurt. She understood his feelings, in a way. He was uncomfortable with her; he didn't know when to be a friend and when a stepfather. She knew she was being unreasonable, but some angry impulse drove her on. He might try to understand *me,* she thought resentfully. He was so clumsy with her.

One evening Mother came into her room and sat on the bed

with a thoughtful frown. She had a folded sheet of paper in her hand. She paused uncertainly for a moment, then she said, "Today I got your report from Kenner, dear. I thought you might like to see it."

The report was very different from any Sheila had received from her other school.

SHEILA DAVIS

Sheila is a very withdrawn, brooding girl with a well-developed fantasy-life. To some extent this is normal for her age, poised between childhood and adolescence. Her egocentricity on one occasion took the more healthy form of exhibitionism, when she was rather a hit in a school play. Since then, however, she has been extremely self-absorbed, except for one healthy excursion into mischief organized by other children.

(Sheila was interested to find that rather embarrassing incident described as "healthy.")

She is obviously preoccupied by family problems still not resolved emotionally. She has, however, responded fairly favorably in class.

Rosalie Dennis
English Teacher

One typhoid shot, September: $5.00. No illness.

Mildred Hobbs
Nurse

We are not worried about Sheila; we
feel she needs time and patience to
develop in her own way. She is still
getting the "feel" of the school, and
is not yet used to an atmosphere so
different from that of her previous
school. Considering her former education and her own personality, Sheila's
reaction to Kenner so far is perfectly
satisfactory. We are pleased to have
her with us.

                            Bianca Kenner
                          William Kenner

"Well!" Sheila exclaimed, a little disturbed by Rosalie's com-
ments but pleasantly surprised by the Kenners'. "Maybe I
didn't get on so badly as I thought."

Mother looked at her for a moment, frowning. Then she
spoke in a firm, decided tone.

"I've been thinking it over, dear, and I realize now it was a
mistake to send you to that school. You don't seem to have
gotten anything out of it; Kenner just isn't the place for you.
Some people need discipline and routine more than others to
keep active. I guess you're one of those."

"But Mother, I hate routine; it bores me to death. I'm not
bored by Rosalie's English class. It's fun, and interesting."

"Maybe so." Mother looked doubtful. "But is that enough?"

"No." Of course it wasn't enough.

"Well, then. I'm going to start investigating some other
schools. Perhaps a day school would be best, after all. You can
change next autumn.

"Okay," said Sheila indifferently.

When Mother had gone, Sheila sat thinking. In a few days she
would be back at Kenner. Was the next term going to be just

like the last? She was beginning to fear Kenny would *never* advise her. If she were going to do anything, she'd better start making up her mind right now. Reading and daydreaming just weren't enough.

Well then. She would study singing with Jeanne Dupont. She didn't have a voice like Sally's and never would; but she liked to sing, so she *would* sing. Since she didn't like sports she'd try modern dance. And chemistry: Jerry had said Kenny was a stimulating teacher.

She would learn to play folk songs on the guitar. Mimi, who'd rather given up on it (she said F major was too difficult), had offered to lend Sheila her guitar and her book of chord instructions.

She would learn to read music.

And she would produce some plays herself, and act in them.

Those were her New Year's resolutions. For the last few days of the holidays she and Stan got on fairly well.

Chapter Nine

"*H*i, Sheila!" Sally turned when Sheila came into their room, the first evening back at school. Sally had arrived earlier. "Did you have a nice holiday? . . . Sheila! What a *fabulous* coat!" She came over and stroked it, envious and admiring. "Is it mink?"

"Just muskrat."

"Oh. Well, it's gorgeous anyway. Look what I brought back for our room." On Sally's dresser was a small aquarium; two angelfish swam inside. "Aren't they lovely? Their names are Willy and Bianca." Sally smiled impishly. "I hope you're not allergic to *fish!*"

Her tone was completely friendly; Sheila was amazed. Later she learned that Sally had made a New Year's resolution to like her. Having made it, Sally at once did like her, simply and completely, as though she always had.

"I got Pop to drive me, since it seemed safer than taking my fish on the train. I left my darling baby boy home this time; country life wasn't doing him much good. He's still vicious, but drawing-room vicious, not stable-vicious. He just attacks people, not other cats."

Sheila was pleased to know that The Cat of Cats would no longer be at Kenner.

"Hey, kids!" Mimi burst into the room, heavily laden as

usual. "Have you heard the news? I just got it from Jack and Gaby—"

"Haven't you noticed Sheila's fabulous coat?" Sally interrupted.

"Of course, I've been drooling over it on the train. . . . What was I saying? Oh! Guess what?"

The other two couldn't think what.

"Oh, come on, try and guess."

"Nice or awful?" Sally asked.

"Mainly awful—but *interesting*."

"Rosalie got married and decided to settle down and raise a family of her own to psychoanalyze," Sheila suggested jokingly.

"Sheila! You're a genius!"

"You mean, she did?"

"No, but it's true she's not coming back. She had hepatitis or something, and the doctor says she needs a long time to convalesce. He seems to think teaching us is a very exhausting job, but I can't think why, can you? Poor Rosalie! I guess she must be very delicate."

Somehow Sheila couldn't see Rosalie Dennis as delicate.

"So, anyway," Mimi went on, "we're going to have a new teacher, but just for English. And—guess what? It's a man!"

The other two were very intrigued.

"Well!" said Sheila. "That'll be an interesting change."

"What's he like?" Sally asked eagerly.

"His name is Nicholas Rutherford—isn't it divine? I do hope he won't want us to call him 'Nick' or 'Nicky'; Nicholas is such a great name, it's a pity to shorten it. Anyway, he's *English*. He used to know Kenny when she went to college in London, and I bet that means he's an old boy friend. He used to teach at a boys' school in England, but he got tired of it and came to Canada to travel and write a novel. It seems he doesn't really want to teach again, he inherited money or something; but when poor darling, delicate Rosalie suddenly couldn't come back, he agreed to help the Kenners out for the rest of the year. Imagine—an English schoolmaster teaching *us!*"

The other two girls were excited by the news. They had never cared for Rosalie the way Mimi did; and a man teacher promised at least an interesting diversion.

But Sally was a bit uneasy. "I hope he won't be too terribly old-fashioned. What if he starts caning the boys? They might fight back. At least I *hope* they'd fight back."

"Surely the Kenners will have told him how to teach us," Sheila protested.

"Oh, no," said Sally. "All the teachers here teach in their own way; the Kenners believe in letting them find their own methods."

Mimi added, "Ordinarily they'd have got somebody progressive, but this is kind of a last-minute thing, I guess. I just hope he won't be too horribly pe*dantic*."

They went into English the next morning filled with curiosity. Mr. Rutherford had been introduced to the school at breakfast, and they liked his looks. He was about forty, tall and thin, with a long narrow face, iron-gray hair, and a pale brown skin. He wore just the right kind of well-cut but worn tweeds they felt a traditional Englishman should wear. They were only disappointed that he didn't have an academic gown.

He had arranged the chairs in the English room in neat rows—a bad sign. But he smiled pleasantly when they entered and sat down. He didn't sit on the sofa, like Rosalie; he stood before the window. On the nearby table was a neat pile of crisp new books.

"Is everybody here? Well, I'll take a roll call and see."

"A *roll* call?" said Mike incredulously. "Oh—sorry, of course you just want to get to know our names."

"That's right." Mr. Rutherford gave him a faint smile. He called out their names, and everybody said, "Here." Pierre said, "*Ici*," for variety.

"Now"—Mr. Rutherford put the list of names back in his pocket—"let me make one thing clear from the start. I don't know what methods Rosalie Dennis used in teaching you, and I don't want to know. I am not Rosalie Dennis. I intend to handle this class in my own way. One thing I dislike is absence. You may be warned now that I intend to give tests two or three times a week—sometimes without warning."

They were all speechless. He smiled reassuringly.

"Now, don't look so dismayed. So long as you do your preparation each night you won't find the tests difficult. But enough of mundane matters. Now, tell me what you read last term."

Gaby spoke up first, so the others fell quiet. "*Hamlet* and *Finnegans Wake* and the complete poetic works of Ogden Nash."

"Gabrielle Newman, isn't it?" He frowned at her. "Gabrielle, are you trying to have me on?"

"What?" Gaby was puzzled. "I don't know what you mean."

"She wasn't kidding, if *that's* what you mean," Mike said coldly. "Those are the things we read."

"Michael"—(well, he has a quick memory for names, anyway, Sheila thought; you have to hand him that)—"will you please address me as 'Mr. Rutherford'—or 'sir,' if you prefer. I am considerably older than you and, I think, wiser. I expect a certain amount of respectful consideration from my pupils."

His words were pompous, but his manner was not. His voice was good-natured, his faint smile almost friendly. They

113

couldn't decide how much they ought to resent what he said. They were suspicious and wary.

"All right, now. *Hamlet, Finnegans Wake,* Ogden Nash. Emily, which of these works would you say was the greatest?"

"*Finnegans Wake,*" Mimi replied without hesitation, "because it's all in the subconscious. And it's funny."

"It's funny all right, but not the greatest—" Ben began, but Mr. Rutherford broke in.

"Please raise your hand before speaking. Never mind now, but another time."

"Raise my . . . Oh. Well, anyway, *Hamlet* isn't *funny,* but it's a greater work of literature because Shakespeare was such a great genius. I mean, he wrote so many plays. And he's so—so *subtle.* I never dreamed Hamlet had an Oedipus complex till Rosalie pointed it out. Now, if I wrote a play about a guy like Hamlet, people would guess it right away."

"Sheila, can you explain Hamlet's Oedipus complex to me?"

"Oh, dear," Sheila murmured, wishing he'd asked anything but that. "Well . . ." She pulled herself together. "It's kind of confusing . . . Hamlet identifies with his father so he hates his uncle . . . No, he identifies with his *uncle* and he's jealous of . . . No, wait, he's angry at his *mother* because . . ." She gave up. "I'm sorry. I just can't."

"Gabrielle, can you tell me why *Hamlet* is such a great tragedy?"

Gaby was insulted at being asked such an easy question.

"Because they all die in the end, of course."

The class were growing more hostile. They suspected Mr. Rutherford of deliberately trying to make them look foolish.

Tony burst out, "Do *you* know why *Hamlet* is such a great tragedy? . . . sir?"

Mr. Rutherford was taken aback. He stiffened slightly. Everyone waited expectantly for his reply. Finally he gave them a rueful little smile.

"Well, I must admit, after twenty years of teaching *Hamlet,* I still find its total meaning somewhat mysterious."

They smiled, relaxing a little. Maybe he wasn't so bad after all. But they hadn't made up their minds yet. He was still on trial.

"What do you think of Ogden Nash, Pierre?" Mr. Rutherford asked.

"He's fun," said Pierre. "Not as funny as *Finnegans Wake,* though."

"I'm afraid I'm not too familiar with Mr. Nash's work. Gerald, will you come forward and distribute these books to the class? This will be your poetry text for the term."

"Text?" Janet murmured, puzzled. Jerry went forward and passed around the books, which were anthologies of English poetry.

"All right, children. This term we shall read selections from *The Canterbury Tales, David Copperfield—*"

"I've read that—"

"I'd rather read something modern—"

"You will raise your hands before speaking. And you will allow me to decide what you shall read."

"But Rosalie Dennis always—"

"I'm not interested in what Rosalie Dennis did. Now, tonight I want you to read the odes of Keats in your poetry text. Decide which you like best, and choose two or more stanzas to memorize. Tomorrow you'll recite them in class."

Mimi stared at him incredulously. But she remembered to raise her hand.

"Yes, Emily?"

"Did you say *memorize?* . . . To re*cite?*"

"I did," he said pleasantly.

"But . . . that's pe*dantic!*"

"What is, Emily?"

"Learning by rote. Rosalie says—"

"I don't want to hear her name mentioned again in this room."

"But—"

"Emily, if you continue to argue, I will ask you to memorize the *whole* poem."

Mimi shut up. But afterward, out in the corridor, she exploded with the others. Imagine, reciting! How pointless and pedantic! They longed for Rosalie again. Even Pierre decided he hadn't fully appreciated her before, and now it was too late.

As the first week went by, things got worse and worse. Mr. Rutherford assigned passages from *The Canterbury Tales* to be memorized, as well as many more poems. Those who refused were unable to do the tests. Mr. Rutherford had a positive genius for springing a test on you when you least expected it. The tests were short and a lot easier than Rosalie's famous one. But the pupils were resentful. They felt they were not being allowed to follow their own interests and tastes, that they were given work for work's sake. They rebelled; they sulked; they argued; and they were only given more assignments and more tests. They began cutting classes more and more frequently. By the end of the second week the class was never more than half full.

A very cold spell had set in; one night it went down to forty below zero. The heating, previously at a minimum, was turned up; in every fireplace fires blazed day and night. A few minutes outdoors—bundled thickly, scarves over mouths—and noses, toes, and fingers were numb. Gaby liked to rub her feet along the shabby living room carpet and then touch people, laughing when they jumped at the small electric shock. In the evenings Mr. Rutherford's English students (fifteen in all, nearly half the school) gathered before the library fire, toasting marshmallows and complaining about him. The seventeen who weren't taking English listened at first with interest and sympathy, later with boredom. "After all," Ian pointed out, "you don't have to go to class. So why all the fuss?"

"Now, that's what I call a really awful, apathetic, irresponsible attitude," Mimi exclaimed indignantly. "Just because *you* don't care about anything but science! Gee, we *like* English—I mean, we used to. It was the most popular course in the school, and now this Rutherford creep is wrecking it. He shouldn't be allowed to get away with it."

Jerry, of course, argued in Mr. Rutherford's favor, to uphold his reputation as the school conservative. He wasn't completely insincere, for he did genuinely respect the new English teacher. He admired his ability to keep calm no matter how trying his students became. The more argumentative they were, the calmer he grew. Occasionally a steely note crept into his voice, but he never lost his temper. At the same time, even Jerry had to admit that English with Rosalie had been a lot more fun.

"You know, I'm beginning to miss old Phil," Mike said. "Things were lively when he was around." (Already Mike was forgetting how bored he had grown with Phil's breakages.) "You never knew when you'd hear a crash—and then there was the suspense of wondering, 'Which window this time?' Gee, this term is turning into the dullest since I first came to the school. Nobody seems to be inspired to write songs or plays or anything. Last Saturday we didn't even *have* an entertainment."

"Yeah, something's wrong this term," Ian agreed. "Last term

was great, but this term just seems to have started badly somehow. I don't know why."

"It's Nicholas Rutherford," Mimi declared grimly. "He's an evil omen."

To try and liven things up a bit, Willy started a series of Friday-evening lectures. He posted a list of topics in the front hall:

LECTURE SERIES

1) What Is Art?

2) Psychology of the French-Canadian Novel.

3) The New Democratic Party: What Now?

4) True Facts about Nuclear Warfare.

5) The Historic St. Lawrence (colored slides).

6) Is It Wrong to Tell Lies?

All subject to last-minute cancellation if less
    than six people show up

Many did go to the lectures. But the general atmosphere of the school remained less lively than usual. At Sunday meetings the English students complained about the new teacher to the Kenners. (Mr. Rutherford never came. He evidently didn't dare, knowing his unpopularity with nearly half the school.) The Kenners listened politely, but they weren't at all helpful.

"I think you're exaggerating," said Kenny at the fourth meeting. "He may not be an ideal teacher, but it was kind of him to agree to help us out when Rosalie left so suddenly. It's only for the rest of the year. I think you ought to give him more of a chance."

There were murmurs of agreement from Willy, Jeanne, Jerry, and from the seventeen students not taking English.

Ben spoke up boldly. "Well, *I* think Nicholas Rutherford should be dismissed."

"No!" said Liz, who wasn't taking English. "The poor guy's only been here four weeks."

"But *we're* the ones who have him as a teacher! What right have you to decide he should stay?"

"My vote is as good as yours. I *might* decide to take English. What I mean is, this isn't just a matter for you English students; it's a question of general school policy, and we should all have equal say."

The opposition numbered twenty-one altogether—against the fourteen English students (not counting Jerry). A comfortable majority to veto getting rid of Mr. Rutherford.

"Democracy!" Dick grumbled. "Sometimes I'd almost prefer an enlightened dictatorship."

"By 'enlightened' I assume you mean a dictator who'd think exactly as you do," Willy teased.

"No, I do *not* mean somebody like me—I mean *me*, period. Boy, you'd soon see some big changes around here!"

The complaints made Sheila feel again rather out of things. For she was so much happier now than she had been last term, it was difficult to understand that everyone didn't feel the same way. How odd to realize it wasn't that school itself had improved but that she had changed.

She was busy now. She sang songs in French and English with Jeanne, who was irritable but encouraging. "You have a nice little voice," she told her, at the first meeting. "We shall now work to make it bigger! Your breathing— *Mon Dieu Seigneur, c'est terrible!* You breathe in little gasps, from the throat. You must learn to breathe from deep, deep down." She held Sheila's hands against her diaphragm. "Feel it down here—draw it deep and slow, so. . . . If you will learn how to breathe, and expand your voice, maybe you will develop a nice little musical-comedy talent, *oui?*"

As a singing teacher, Jeanne was a little bird with a big voice, ruffly blouses emphasizing her large bosom, skirts tight, thin ankles wobbling upon very high heels. In the modern-dance class, bounding around the room in a purple leotard, she was a bit comical. Her instructions were vague, as she believed in freedom of expression; so nobody paid much attention. She was particularly annoyed by Mimi and Sally. Mimi was energetic and imaginative, but awkward; Sally was graceful but restrained, coolly ignoring Jeanne's urgings to let herself go. The only boy in the class was Ben. He was taking it to try to impress Sally, whom he suspected of losing interest in him. Ben spent most of the time clowning and trying to make the others laugh. The more exasperated Jeanne became, the more mischievous he was. She was pleased with Sheila, though. "Relax," she kept saying irritably at first. "Let yourself go!" But as the term wore on, she began to praise her.

Then there was chemistry with Kenny—the experiments fun, the theory sometimes difficult. And at the last moment she had also decided to take modern European history with Willy because Sally recommended it. "It's fun—he teaches very dramatically," Sally told her; and Sheila, so pleased by Sally's new friendliness, joined the class. Willy's way of "dramatizing" the Napoleonic wars was to have the class go outdoors and crawl around in the snow on their bellies to try and get an idea of what Napoleon's soldiers had gone through during the Russian Campaign. Sheila caught her first cold of the year after that class. But she liked Willy; he was a favorite with many of his students.

In her spare time Sheila did little outside reading these days. She had adopted Mimi's guitar and was learning chords. She was proud of the calluses already forming on her left fingertips. Mimi and Sally sometimes asked her to play while they sang. "Okay," she would agree, "but please sing very slowly." She had mastered an interminably slow version of "Greensleeves," which drove them mad: "A-las, my . . . lo-ove, you . . . do . . . me . . . wrong . . ." She liked the minor chords best.

Sometimes Sheila was amazed at herself. She couldn't understand it. What had happened to her? All she had done was spend a whole term feeling horribly bored and lonely—so much so that she had finally decided to take some courses out of sheer desperation for something to do. And then, all of a sudden, she seemed to wake up, to be interested in things, to enjoy them. How could such a small decision have changed her so much? It was all very strange. But it was wonderful. No longer did Mimi's and Sally's activities seem mysterious. Now Sheila was as busy as they. She didn't have time to write any more long, detailed letters to Daddy. She sent him the same brief notes she sent Mother.

Mimi, usually involved in many things at once, was rather idle this term. Two of her favorite courses—psychology and comparative religion—weren't being given for the present, since her beloved Rosalie had gone. "And I've taken all Willy's best courses already," she mourned. She was taking biology but found she hated to dissect pickled worms. "I look down at the poor little thing, all disemboweled and helpless, and I think, 'There, but for the grace of God . . .'" She complained about Mr. Rutherford more than anybody, yet she went to nearly every class. "Every day I swear I won't," she tried to justify herself to her roommates, "but after breakfast I feel kind of bored and uninspired, and somehow I end up wandering over to the English room." She was often as much as half an hour late; yet still she went.

Sally was busy with French literature, German, aesthetics,

and first aid. Between classes she spent long hours in the art studio, painting an apple and an orange in a bowl. She painted them five times, with careful realism, seeking some mysterious kind of perfection. The fruit grew moldy, even smelly, but she wouldn't let anybody throw them out. While she agreed with the complaints about Mr. Rutherford, she couldn't be bothered with worrying much over him herself. After the first week, deciding English was a drag this term, she simply dropped the class altogether.

But Sheila, while she didn't enjoy English nearly as much as she had with Rosalie, was too cheerful about life in general to mind the way the others did. She was intoxicated by this mysterious change in herself. If she was busy with something interesting, she would cut English; if not, she would go. She was curious to see what would happen.

The only one of her resolutions still unfulfilled was the most important one: to act in another play.

"Since nobody's written any new plays," she suggested hopefully to a group by the library fire, "why don't we choose some play in one of the drama books and produce it?"

Nobody liked this idea.

"We *always* do our own plays."

"Doing an original play for the first time is half the fun."

"Each entertainment is a world première."

Sally came to the rescue with a suggestion.

"What about a variety show? We could put it on later in the term. Different people could think up something short: a couple of songs by Mike, a skit by Mimi, a ballet by Angela— And Bill can do his comic imitations . . ."

"I've got a great one of old Ruthy," Bill put in.

"Great! And Tony can compose something short. . . . And somebody might improvise poetry on-the-spot to Sheila's guitar, if she can learn to play a bit faster. And Dick can do his magic tricks."

"Everybody's seen them. Everybody knows how they're done."

"Well, he can learn some more. And Pierre can show his movie, if it's finished in time."

"Not till summer," said Pierre. "I want to film the spring floods."

"I've got another idea," Mimi exclaimed suddenly. "Let's have a fashion show. Everybody who's tall and slim and has lots of nice new clothes can be in it."

"Which means *you*," said Sally. "But why not? You modeling your new clothes can be one of the numbers."

They all agreed that a variety show wasn't a bad idea. As the days went by more and more numbers were thought of—until Sheila feared a six-hour marathon with no audience but the staff. But the English students were still preoccupied with their new teacher. Entertainments were familiar; Mr. Rutherford was still a novelty and an irritation.

Mimi, to demonstrate her scorn for pedantic learning by rote, recited poetry in an exaggerated mechanical singsong: "The *cur*-few *tolls* the *knell* of *par*-ting *day* . . ." Mr. Rutherford paid no attention.

Ben said "Mr. Rutherford, sir" as often as possible: "Please, Mr. Rutherford, sir, do you think Chaucer's Knight, Mr. Rutherford, sir, is a realistic character, Mr. Rutherford, sir?" Mr. Rutherford didn't seem to notice.

Pierre wrote flippant answers to questions in the tests: *Is Dickens as sensitive a portrayer of human nature as Chaucer? Why, sure!* Mr. Rutherford handed back his papers without comment.

Gaby hummed "Alouette" over and over again very softly all

through a test, and the others joined in. Mr. Rutherford praised their harmony.

Mike caught a rat and set it loose in class. Rachel had hysterics and was quickly removed. Mr. Rutherford looked bored.

Psychological warfare, as Pierre called these tactics, didn't seem to have any effect on the new teacher. He seemed hoplessly set in his ways, totally incapable of accepting any criticism.

"Why not quit completely, like Sally?" Jerry asked Mike one morning at breakfast. "I don't understand it. You keep complaining about old Rutherford, but you keep *going*. It doesn't make sense."

"Well . . ." Mike seemed a bit embarrassed by this question. "We just want to see what this Rutherford's capable of, how far he'll go. Oh, one of these days I'll cut the class for good," he vowed firmly. However, as the days went by, although Mike sometimes skipped English class for a whole week, he always returned. And so did the others, except for Sally. Classes dwindled to three or four students at a time. Mr. Rutherford marked down the daily absences in his notebook but made no comment. Jerry, of course, was always present.

At the same time that the classes were growing smaller, a sense of tension was building. Jerry had to admit to himself that he was rather enjoying the situation. In a way it was fun to be Mr. Rutherford's sole supporter. But sometimes he was sorry there was nobody to appreciate his loyalty. After all, Mr. Rutherford saw him only in class; and Jerry had—in a weak moment—joined in the "Alouette" incident—for purely musical motives. He had a nice harmony in his mind which he just couldn't resist adding. Mr. Rutherford didn't hear the library arguments, when Jerry stuck up for him. It seemed sad that poor old Ruthy didn't know he had a supporter. Calm though he appeared, he must feel frustrated sometimes and perhaps lonely.

Playing hockey one afternoon, Jerry saw Mr. Rutherford watching. An exciting match was in progress. The players, in their brightly colored caps, sweaters, and stockings, speeded around the rink under a white winter sky, and the flashing blades of their skates cut swirling patterns in the ice. The rink was always clear, for Jerry devotedly swept and shoveled after each snowfall; the rest of the frozen river was like a smooth white field. Jerry was captain of one team, Liz of the other. Brandishing her hockey stick with wild war cries, cheeks glowing, her breath a thick white puff in the icy air, Liz was a fearsome sight. She wore several heavy sweaters, and her feet, in dirty-white fancy skates, looked too tiny to support so large a bulk. But she played a fast, accurate game.

"Good going, George!" she cried as the school's best hockey player scored another goal. Naturally Liz had bagged George Novotny for her team. Jerry's own team had won only two games this term. But he was enjoying hockey at Kenner. There was no stopping to argue over rules; it was far too cold. You had to keep moving.

Liz's team won, as usual. Jerry had several good players, but he also had Mimi. She *would* play every single day.

When Jerry came off the rink and removed his skates, he saw Mr. Rutherford again.

"Hello, sir! How did you like our game?"

"It's an exciting game—ice hockey. Looks rather dangerous, though."

"Well, most of the kids *are* pretty bruised by now—and a few cuts. Especially Mimi Holly; she falls down all the time. Liz and I tossed a coin over whose team she'd be on, and I lost."

They walked up the hill toward the building. A silence fell. Jerry was suddenly shy.

"You know, sir," he burst out, "a lot of the kids don't like your teaching methods, but I do. I mean, Rosalie Dennis was more fun in some ways, but you're giving us a more well-rounded education. Better for getting into college and all that."

Mr. Rutherford smiled. He had a nice smile.

"Naturally I'm aware that you're my sole supporter. After all, you're known as the school conservative, aren't you?"

Jerry was somewhat squashed. Mr. Rutherford seemed more amused than grateful, as though Jerry's defense of him were as childish as the others' complaints.

The following Saturday was the most beautiful day of winter. The temperature had risen to ten above; the wind was still, the air crisp; the sun shone brightly from a vivid blue sky, the snow was a dazzling white. At breakfast Liz made an announcement.

"Today I thought it'd be fun to go on a cross-country ski trip. Willy will drive us up to the ski hill, and we'll ski down and take a roundabout route home across the fields. Okay? So anybody who wants to come, meet in front at nine o'clock."

"Good old Liz," Pierre murmured, almost affectionately. "She really does have good ideas."

"She's okay, I guess," said Jerry grudgingly. But he found himself eager to go. What about class? Liz had no classes today, so she wouldn't be cutting anything. Jerry had only English. From the conversations around him, he gathered that all the other English students intended to go with Liz. Nearly everyone in the school had skis.

What should he do? As Mr. Rutherford's sole supporter, he ought to go to class. But Mr. Rutherford hadn't seemed too grateful for Jerry's loyalty. Very well, then, Jerry decided, he would go with the skiers.

Liz seemed surprised to find twenty-five people gathered

outside the front door at nine with their skis. Noticing that all the English students were there, she smiled and said, "I guess old Ruthy will have an empty classroom this morning, eh?" She was flattered that her cross-country idea was so popular.

Skis and poles were fastened to the ski rack on top of the bus. Everybody piled in. Willy got into the driver's seat, and they started off.

They turned away from the frozen river, passed the hotel, the railway station, the post office, and began to climb. The scene was familiar, as during the winter term Willy often took groups of students to the ski hill on weekends. They passed woods, fields, and many houses, for the growing village was spreading upward toward the mountain. They saw many apple trees, dark and twisted in their winter nakedness. The ski hill rose up steeply; a section of mountainside had been cleared, so there was now a broad, smooth white strip. Willy let them off and drove back to school.

Sally and Ben would have preferred to stay and ski on the hill all morning; Liz was firm. "We came along to go on a cross-country trip," she insisted, "and on a cross-country trip we'll go. Wait and see, kids—it's fun, and you keep nice and warm."

Across the white fields, barns and farmhouses were quiet, as though asleep, but smoke came drifting thinly out of chimneys. It was fun skiing down leisurely slopes; but as the ground became flatter, some of the skiers began to tire. Liz led the way, sliding her skis along at a steady pace, climbing expertly over wire fences, warm and glowing. After a couple of miles Gaby fell farther and farther behind, a forlorn red-and-blue figure against the vast expanse of white.

"Slow down a bit, Liz," Rachel urged. "Wait for Gaby."

"What's wrong with you kids?" Liz was disgusted. "You didn't *have* to come, you know."

"But it's a long way, and still at least five more miles."

"So what? Look, I didn't suggest we go for a brief stroll, did I? I *said* 'cross country.' "

"You didn't say how *far* across the country."

"Well, what d'you think 'cross country' means, anyway? Across a field or two? Actually, I wanted to continue all day, but I decided to go easy on you lazy things."

"Oh, dear, Liz really is a drag sometimes," Mimi murmured to Sheila. "She used to be a lot more fun."

"Didn't she always organize things?" Sheila asked. She had heard that Liz had been at Kenner since the age of ten, but couldn't imagine her ever having been very different.

"Yes, but she was kind of mischievous. When I first came to the school, she was thirteen, and she used to dare people to do dangerous things, like climbing difficult trees. And she used to organize raids on the kitchen at night, after Madame had gone home and locked it. Gaby wasn't around then to pick the lock; so Liz would lead a group of kids onto the roof and we'd climb down the kitchen chimney into the old fireplace. But then she suddenly got all responsible and hung up on physical fitness. Oh, well," she decided tolerantly, "I guess it's just another stage."

A road was visible from where they stood. Peering with his farsighted eyes, Jerry saw a splotch which looked like a Coca-Cola sign. "Hey, that must be a store or a restaurant or something. Let's go in and take a rest. I'm hungry, anyway."

"It'll be harder to keep on once we've stopped," Liz warned, the voice of experience. But popular demand was so great she had to agree. They would have abandoned her otherwise.

The building, which had a large peeling Coca-Cola sign on one wall, was neither a restaurant nor a store, but a farmhouse. However, they were near a village; so they continued along the road. The village was just a long narrow line of houses along one street, plus a garage, an immense church, and a tiny store. They all took off their skis and entered the store.

It was extremely warm and stuffy; an ancient Quebec heater stood in the middle of the main room. Shelves on the walls were filled with an assortment of things to buy—magazines, candy, cookies, Halloween masks, blue jeans, aprons, lipstick, house-coats, crucifixes, little statues of the Virgin, nylons, tools, plastic toys, film, can openers, mittens, needles, flypaper, mousetraps, rat poison—all jumbled together with many other things and, oddly, six pairs of cheap boxing gloves.

"Say!" Jerry exclaimed excitedly. "My uncle gave me some boxing lessons once. Any of you boys box?"

None of them ever had, but they urged him to teach them. Jerry had never been very fond of this sport; but here, at last, was something which could be done at Kenner without girls. He offered to give lessons to anybody interested. Six boys bought the six pairs of gloves immediately—after some argument, as all eleven boys present wanted them. The saleslady, a short, stout woman, finally decided who should have them, to prevent a fight. Gaby wanted to buy some too; but, to Jerry's relief, the saleswoman paid no attention to her.

They all bought Cokes and chocolate bars, and idled around, munching, trying on the masks, talking, and generally putting off the inevitable re-entrance into the cold outdoors and the long trip back. The saleswoman leaned against the counter and watched them with rather suspicious interest. Suddenly she frowned deeply and turned to Liz. "You children, you are at de school, *hein? L'école Anglais?*"

"*Oui. L'école Kenner.*"

"Ah." Now she looked more suspicious. "Why-for you come so far? You run away, *peut-être?*"

"*Non, non—nous sommes* . . . um—we're on a cross-country

ski trip. See?" She pointed out the window, where their skis could be seen standing in a snowbank.

"I t'ink you run away," the woman persisted darkly. "I t'ink I go call Monsieur le Curé, and he telephone your school."

Liz was exasperated. "Of course we haven't run away, Madame! We—go—on—a—cross—country—ski—trip," she said very slowly. *"Comprenez?"*

"You 'ave a boy run away in December, *non?* Your principal, 'e come 'ere look for 'im."

"Oh, yes—Phil. He isn't at the school anymore. He's going to a psychiatrist," Liz said reassuringly. But Madame's eyes narrowed.

"I will not 'ave no guns in my store—*pas du tout.* *Comprenez?"*

"We haven't *got* any guns, Madame, I *promise.* Pas des—des, um, guns."

Sally, whose French was as natural as her English, came forward to explain. Pierre joined her. But Madame seemed even more suspicious of them.

"What's this about guns?" Jerry asked. Now he remembered some story in the papers a couple of years ago—about a Kenner pupil shooting a teacher.

"Willy got an old rifle once and decided to give some of the kids lessons with a target by the river," Liz explained. "He stood too near the target, and one boy shot him in the leg by accident. A wild story went around that he'd shot Willy on purpose, but really it was just Willy's carelessness."

"Oh." Jerry was rather disappointed.

Madame had vanished suddenly into a back room. "Oh, dear," said Sally, "I think she's going to call the police or the Curé or something."

"Come on, kids," said Liz. "Let's beat it!"

They hastily put on their skis and left the village.

It was terribly cold after their warm rest; the numbing chill seeped into their bones, and the five-mile trip home seemed endlessly far away. They were stuffed full of Coke and chocolate bars. "Chocolate's good for quick energy," Jerry said encouragingly; but it seemed to be taking a while to work. They decided to go along the side of the firm-packed snowy road, as it was quicker than across the fields. Bits of charcoal, sprinkled to prevent cars from slipping, scraped on the bottoms of their skis. Mimi, bored with the road, climbed up on the snowbank. Immediately one ski sank in deeply; she exclaimed "Ow" and sat down.

"Ow! I've twisted my ankle or something; it hurts—*ow!*"

Jerry, who was just ahead, stopped. To her delight he came over to help her. He scraped the snow off her leg, removed the boot from her ski, and carefully took the boot off her foot. Mimi winced slightly, but by now the pain was almost gone. However, enjoying his attention, she played it up. "What'll I do?" she said pitifully. "I can't walk all the way home on it."

"We could go home and send Willy with the car to get you," Liz suggested.

"I'd freeze to death waiting here—and I *won't* go back to that store."

Pierre looked ahead. "Here comes a farm truck. Maybe you can get a ride."

The truck began to slow down even before they hailed. It was driven by a ruddy-faced farmer; beside him sat a tiny, withered old man bundled in scarfs. The open back of the truck was full of rattling milk cans. It stopped; the door opened; the little old man came out. Beneath his coat trailed an ankle-length black gown.

"Oh, dear," Pierre exclaimed, "it's Monsieur le Curé."

The little man came up to them, beaming benevolently, tiny blue eyes twinkling. *"Bonjour, mes enfants! Qu'est-ce que c'est qui passe ici?"*

Pierre and Sally explained the situation. Monsieur le Curé listened, smiling and nodding his head at everything. His benevolent twinkle grew warmer. He apologized for the saleswoman's silly panic and offered to take Mimi and her skis back to school. Everybody was grateful except Mimi. "Gee," she murmured, wishing she hadn't made such a big production of her ankle (it felt perfectly normal now), "I'll feel kind of shy riding with them all by myself when I can't talk to them. They don't know any English and my French is awful. . . . Can't somebody else come too?" She looked at Jerry hopefully.

"There isn't much room," Liz objected.

"Let Gaby go since she's so tired," said Jerry. "She can ride on Mimi's lap."

Mimi glared at Gaby, who accepted thankfully. Their skis were put in the back with the milk cans, they climbed in front and drove away.

"Boy, you sure squashed Mimi," Ben commented. "She was keen for you to go with her."

"Why? I didn't mean to squash her."

"She's got a crush on you, stupid."

"Oh, that," said Jerry indifferently. He really couldn't take Mimi's passion seriously. She just wasn't his type of girl. He liked small, graceful girls who danced well and didn't talk all the time.

Sheila found herself unexpectedly glad to realize that Jerry was not attracted to Mimi. Why am I so glad? she wondered in surprise. Am I getting keen on Jerry too? She had always thought of him as just a very casual friend—though with the added fascination of his being a boy, of course. The romantic heroes of her fantasies weren't at all like Jerry. What were they like? They had always been so dim and shadowy. . . . But she knew they were older, and very sophisticated, and usually blond. Still, Jerry *was* good-looking, in a boy's way, not a man's, and a good dancer too. She was a teenager now; it was high time to get interested in somebody real.

They continued on their way, warming after a while, and even enjoying the rest of the trip—especially as they neared the school, thinking of hot cocoa and apple pie. Jerry smiled at Sheila once, her heart skipped a beat, and her cheeks glowed warmer. Gee, she thought, isn't it funny? I decided I'd be in love with him, and now I *am*. Somehow she couldn't bring herself to describe her feelings as a "crush." It sounded so unromantic and juvenile. All right for Mimi, perhaps; not good enough for herself.

Mr. Rutherford was standing by the window as usual when nine of his English students entered the classroom on Monday. If he was surprised to see such a large turnout (more than there had been since early in the term), he didn't show it. They all wore elaborately casual expressions. Jerry was a little embarrassed by Saturday's absence and sat down at the back of the room. To his surprise, on the table beside Mr. Rutherford were a portable phonograph and an album—"Readings from *The Canterbury Tales.*" Records suggested a fun, easy class, not a test.

When they were all settled, the teacher said, "Today we will listen to selections from *The Canterbury Tales,* but first I have a word of complaint." They all stiffened defensively. "I am growing more than a little weary of the extremely unattractive costume favored by the female members of my class. I realize you're allowed to dress as you like at this school, and I don't object to casualness; but I really must draw the line at downright ugliness. . . ."

The girls at Kenner were extremely fashion-minded. Nobody could say just how a particular fashion started; yet somehow, by the second or third week of each term, a distinct Look could be seen. Last term it had been the Striped Look; this term, the Dirty Look. This involved lank, unwashed hair, dirty navy sweatshirts, dirty jeans over dirty black tights with holes in the heels, and rundown ballet slippers. Mimi tried the hardest, deliberately rolling in the dust under her bed (she had to take a pill afterward because of her allergy to dust). But Sheila, with her naturally greasy hair and rather sallow skin—oily without being pimply—was the most successful. She had just the right "subtly dirty, ingrained quality," as Janet enviously described it, which constituted the current Look.

"I am sure," Mr. Rutherford went on, "that you all possess frocks or skirts of some variety. Before we hear these recordings, you girls will all go to your rooms and put on something with a skirt—a *clean* skirt. And be back in five minutes or you'll be given extra work."

Protesting furiously, the girls left the room. In the hallway Janet stopped.

"Girls, we can't let him get away with this. He didn't criticize the *boys'* clothes at all! It's not fair."

"Well, they're having kind of a clean-cut look this term," Gaby pointed out. "Mike finally cut his hair."

"I know, but it's still unfair; we're supposed to wear what we *want!* Shall we just cut class, or what?"

"Let's do something better," said Mimi. "Something that'll *show* him."

"I know!" said Sheila. "Let's put on skirts—*clean* ones, like he said—over our jeans. I mean, without rolling up the legs or anything."

"Brilliant, Sheila!" Janet exclaimed. "Gee, you're so different this term, I can't believe it. We used to call you the Bookworm."

"Really?" Sheila was surprised to learn that even last term, without realizing it, she had been Somebody.

When the girls returned, their faces carefully deadpan, Mr. Rutherford looked at them without comment. The class passed quite pleasantly, without any reference to Saturday's absence. He's decided to play it cool, Jerry decided, and say nothing.

They listened to a strange voice reading the Chaucer they had been studying. It sounded like a foreign language. Mr. Rutherford explained that this was the English which people spoke in Chaucer's day. They practiced reading a few lines themselves, with the original pronunciation. It was fun. For an hour they forgot how pedantic old Ruthy usually was.

Finally he said, very casually, "Tonight's assignment won't be very taxing mentally; but I want it definitely done for tomorrow, or you'll have to finish it in class. You will all write out 'I promise not to be absent from English class again' five hundred times."

"What?"

They ought to have been prepared for something like this, knowing Ruthy; but his nice behavior for the past hour had put them off their guard. Still, even for him, writing out lines was going a bit too far.

"That's *worse* than pedantic—it's—it's out*rageous* . . . *five hundred times!*"

"On separate lines," the teacher added calmly. "And neatly, or you'll have to do them over."

"But—that's the most pedantic thing I've ever *heard*. Rosalie wouldn't *dream—*"

"One thousand lines for *you*, Emily."

Mimi stormed out of the room in a fury. The others were almost as angry. Even Jerry thought old Ruthy might have thought up a more constructive punishment. Writing lines was an insult to one's dignity.

"This is the last straw," Dick declared. "Simply not writing the lines won't be enough. We must do something decisive."

"Yes," said Janet. "We've *got* to get rid of him. It's all very well for the other kids and the Kenners to be in the majority, but they don't *take* English! *We* should have the right to decide if our own teacher isn't fit to teach us. It's only *fair*. Maybe we can persuade them now."

"No," said Pierre thoughtfully, "that isn't the way to handle it. This is between Ruthy and us, and he never comes to Sunday meetings. It's high time we just dropped the class completely— all of us. So far we haven't made any impression on him. An empty classroom ought to do the trick. With no students at all, he'll have no choice but to resign—of his own free will."

"A *thousand* lines!" Mimi exclaimed. "It's in*human*."

"Okay, then," said Mike, "we'll go on strike for good. I'm sure the others who didn't come today will agree. Sally's on strike already."

Jerry was tempted to go along with the rest. He'd feel an awful fool, being the only one in class. Especially as Mr. Rutherford hadn't seemed too impressed when Jerry told him of his loyalty that day. But old Ruthy would think him even more childish, surely, if after that declaration he didn't stick by him now. So Jerry took a deep breath and announced: "Okay, then, do what you like. I'm going to write out the five hundred lines and go to class as usual."

They were shocked. Nobody had minded Jerry's arguments in Ruthy's favor before because of his reputation as the school conservative. But this was going too far. Ruthy would still have somebody to teach instead of the empty classroom he deserved. Why, he might not even resign! It wouldn't be the only class with a single student.

"Oh, Jerry," Janet exclaimed reproachfully, "how *could* you?"

"I have to," he said, rather embarrassed. He almost regretted his bold decision, but it was too late to turn back now.

Mimi was dismayed. Why had she agreed with the others so unthinkingly? If she hadn't, she might have shared with her adored Jerry the distinction of being Ruthy's only students. But Sheila looked at him with admiration. It didn't matter that he was wrong; he had courage, anyway.

The others were so annoyed they hardly bothered to argue. It was obvious that he was not going to change his mind. The strike would have to be an incomplete one. They were very cold to him. In the dormitory that evening Mike and Pierre ignored Jerry completely. The other two boys, who didn't take English, were more tolerant.

Next morning the English students took care to be very busy during the period of Mr. Rutherford's class. This made the strike a more positive thing, somehow, than if they had just loafed around. Sheila practiced guitar chords. Mimi dropped into Willy's first-aid class. Ben and Mike boxed in the stable. Pierre and Gaby made collages in the art studio.

And Jerry went to English class.

When he came out, he found Mike and Pierre waiting for him. They couldn't contain their curiosity any longer.

"How did it go? What did he say?"

"We had a very nice class," Jerry replied smugly, feeling very mature. "I gave him my lines, and he threw the paper away. Then we listened to more records and talked about the English language. I'm supposed to do a research essay on it for next Monday."

"But what did he say about *us*? About none of us being there?"

"Nothing."

"Nothing?"

"Nothing at all. It was like he didn't even notice."

Jerry smiled and walked away; the others felt a distinct sense of anticlimax. So far, their decisive action seemed to have fallen flat.

Chapter Ten

Sheila sat waiting on the hall bench, but she was too excited to sit still. For once she was wearing a dress—under her fur coat. Daddy was in Montreal for a few days on business, and today he had borrowed a car to come out and visit her.

Mimi, Sally, and a few other girls hovered nearby, chatting on the stairs, curious to see Sheila's handsome father. She would introduce them, of course; but she wasn't going to let any of them come along to lunch. She wanted Daddy to herself.

When the doorbell rang, she jumped up, but Kenny came out of her study and opened the door to him. Daddy looked shorter than Sheila remembered, but maybe it was just that she had grown since her visit to Vancouver in June. His eyes crinkled the same way when he smiled.

"Well, sweetheart, that's quite a coat. You look a sophisticated twenty, doesn't she, Mrs. Kenner?"

Kenny smiled. Sheila said, "It's the one Stan gave me," then remembered the girls hovering on the stairs. After all, Mimi and Sally were her roommates. "Come and meet my father," she urged.

She was interested to observe that while Sally and Janet and the others wore their usual jeans, Mimi had changed into a plaid jumper and white silk blouse. Daddy looked as though he might invite Mimi and Sally along, maybe the Kenners too, but Sheila quickly got him out the door before he had a chance.

"I thought we'd eat at the hotel in St. Hilaire," he said as they climbed into the car, "but it's only twelve and such a lovely day, so how about a drive first?"

"Oh yes!" she said happily.

In the past she and Daddy had gone for long leisurely drives in the country nearly every Sunday. He would entertain her with his funny stories, and she would laugh. And then there had been those other, more recent times, when he had tried to make her understand about himself and Mother getting divorced, and Mother marrying Stan.

The mountain loomed ahead over the flat countryside below. The barren fields were dazzling white in the sun's brightness. They passed through a village—St. Jean Baptiste—and continued on into open country. The roads were white; Daddy drove carefully on the hard-packed snow.

He had been talking about Vancouver—little sketches of new people he had met since moving there. He was a wonderful storyteller. But suddenly his face grew serious. He half turned toward her, with a slight frown.

"You know, sweetheart, the more I hear about this school in your letters, the less I like the sound of it. You don't seem to be learning anything."

"But, Daddy"—she was startled—"I *am!* I *told* you how busy I am this term!"

"Well, history and English and chemistry, yes. But otherwise you just seem to be fooling around."

"But I'm *busy*—"

"How much are you *learning*, Sheila? I must say, I wasn't at all impressed by those girl friends of yours. Mimi was charming; but as for the others, I've never seen a more scruffy-looking bunch of kids in my life. They—well, frankly, they looked positively *dirty*."

Sheila grinned. "But that's *in* this term—the Dirty Look, I mean. Mimi's usually the dirtiest of all; she just put on those clothes to impress you."

He didn't look amused, but still thoughtful. So she added quickly, "Too bad you didn't get to see any of the boys. They're quite clean this term."

He was quiet a moment. Then he said, "I was talking to your mother yesterday; she seems to feel the same way, and regrets her decision to send you here. I agreed with her that it would be a good idea to investigate other schools for next year."

When Mother had spoken of this plan during the holidays, Sheila hadn't cared much one way or the other. Now suddenly the idea of leaving Kenner filled her with dismay. Just when she had finally begun to enjoy herself, to be interested in things!

"But, Daddy, can't you understand? I'm—I'm *happy*," she said helplessly. "Isn't that important?"

"Of course, sweetheart . . . but I doubt if you're learning as much as you should be. That's what school is for, after all."

Sheila sighed with frustration. Why couldn't he understand? He of all people! Suddenly an idea flashed into her mind. Her heart leaped. Deep down, ever since Mother and Stan's marriage, she had had the idea that if things ever got too difficult, she'd save her allowance and run away to Vancouver and live with Daddy. Maybe this was her chance: not to run away secretly, but to go back with him! She wouldn't mind what school she went to if she could live with Daddy in Vancouver.

"Maybe you're right," she said eagerly; "maybe I'm not learning enough. . . . Oh, Daddy, could I go back with you on Friday? To live, I mean. The Kenners wouldn't mind; they're very understanding. And I could go to a day school there, a regular day school, and I'd work very hard. . . . Oh, Daddy, *please!*"

Daddy shook his head decidedly. "Sweetheart, we went over the whole matter before the divorce—you know it's better this way. A girl should be with her mother. You wouldn't have a proper home with me. I'm very difficult to live with—as your mother well knows." His voice was rather bitter; his eyes stared ahead at the white road.

After a glum pause, Sheila asked uneasily, "Daddy . . . will you get married again?"

"*Never* again."

"Mimi says everybody who's divorced remarries at least once."

He grinned suddenly. "That Mimi sounds like a smart girl. But, no, sweetheart. Oh, maybe I will someday—who knows? Mimi may be right. But not for a long time."

Sheila was relieved to hear this. But otherwise she was disappointed in Daddy today. The lovely visit wasn't turning out at all well.

Lunch at the hotel was disappointing too, for Daddy kept coming back to his bad impression of the school. He pointed out the shabbiness of the building—"And don't tell me *that's* just this term's Dirty Look." He said a school on the verge of bankruptcy must be an inferior school; otherwise, rich parents would contribute. (Sheila thought it wisest not to tell him about the Bartells.) When he wasn't criticizing the school, long silences fell between them. It was almost a relief to get back to school, to have coffee with the Kenners in the study.

They didn't talk about school things at all. The three adults discussed differences between western and eastern Canada, pleasantly enough, while Sheila sat silent and rather sullen. She was almost wishing Daddy would go soon.

But when she said good-by to him outdoors, alone, there were sudden tears on her cheeks in the cold air.

"Oh, Daddy! When can I visit you?"

"When the summer holidays begin." He wiped her tears gently with a finger. "The Kenners seem nice, intelligent people, sweetheart; I've nothing against them personally. But I can't help feeling their theories don't work very well in practice. Never mind—we'll decide this summer." He smiled suddenly. "I hope your Variety Show is a success."

When Sheila went soberly to her room, she found Mimi changed back into sweatshirt and jeans, bouncing to the rhythm of loud music on her radio. Sally was painting her toenails with the complete absorption she gave to anything she did, oblivious to the raucous noise.

"Hi, Sheil!" Mimi yelled. "Your father gone?" Sheila nodded. "He isn't *quite* so well preserved as in his picture," Mimi decided critically, "but his deep voice is di*vine.*"

"Yes," Sally agreed, looking up. "I would've liked to talk to him some more."

"Gee, I'm sorry . . . I wish I'd invited you along for lunch," Sheila exclaimed. And suddenly it was true: she did wish they'd been along. It would have been more fun with Mimi and Sally.

Anyway, she was glad she hadn't told Daddy about the strike from English class. The way he felt, he might have taken her out of the school at once.

And so the term wore on.

Jerry's somewhat inexpert boxing lessons were a big hit; he found himself very busy. The boys who didn't have them sent home for boxing gloves. A punching bag was set up in the stable loft. Ben, so small and skinny, with his pale skin and freckles, was remarkably quick and fearless. He gave up modern dance and worked at the punching bag every spare moment. Jerry, who really enjoyed boxing from the side more than in the ring, decided to set himself up as Ben's manager and arrange fights between him and other boys. He got Pierre to take some photographs of Ben posing fiercely with poised gloves. These appeared on large posters distributed throughout the school. Below the picture was written:

KILLER KID DREXLER
vs.
FIGHTING BILLY HINE
Saturday, 3:00 P.M.
Betting Welcome

Poor Louise, who had been looking sickly for some time, finally died—of indigestion, according to Gaby. Mimi discovered her weeping over the plant. "Come, Gaby," she soothed, putting her arm around the smaller girl's shoulders, "let's not leave her like this. We'll bury her in the garden, beside Janet's hamster." They had to clear a lot of snow away and work hard with a pick to dig into the frozen earth. When they had made a small hole, Gaby laid Louise tenderly inside and covered her with hard lumps of earth, still weeping. Mimi had made a tombstone out of a piece of wood. "Just something simple and un—unpretentious," Gaby sobbed; so Mimi painted on it, in black letters:

In Loving Memory of Louise

The Variety Show, performed in March, was a great success. Mimi wasn't feeling very inspired this term, but Pierre had written an amusing bilingual skit in which he played a French doctor and Sheila his English patient. Sheila was again a hit. Willy said she had a good sense of timing, very important in comedy. Mike sang more original folk songs. Mimi, in her one-woman fashion show, revealed all the pretty new clothes she hadn't had a chance to wear this term because of the Dirty Look. It meant long pauses between each outfit while she changed, but Janet filled these in pleasantly with solos on her flute. Mimi as a model was slightly comic, awkwardly imitating poses from *Seventeen;* but the audience enjoyed her number, even the boys. The only flop of evening was Dick, whose new magic tricks didn't work.

The day after, Liz organized another cross-country ski trip— "for people with stamina only." Six went, including Jerry. They got hopelessly lost and were brought back in a tow truck.

Killer Kid Drexler gave Punching Pat L'Anglais a black eye.

One of Sally's fish died. She couldn't tell whether it was Willy or Bianca, so she renamed the survivor "Angel."

Mimi grew a quarter of an inch. "Well, at least I'm slowing down," she said, trying to look on the bright side.

And Jerry continued to go alone to English class. Neither he nor Mr. Rutherford ever made any reference to the prolonged absence of the others. There was a kind of unspoken agreement between them not to. Mr. Rutherford behaved as though a private tutorial with Jerry were the normal thing.

Jerry had no idea whether Ruthy had told the Kenners or Jeanne about the strike. If they did know, they never spoke of it to the students, who made a point of not referring to the matter at Sunday meetings. Even those who had never been in Mr. Rutherford's class thought it best to leave well enough alone; it wasn't their business. The strikers themselves, whenever they passed Mr. Rutherford, muttered a curt "Hello" and generally avoided him as much as possible.

Kenner School Presents:

A Variety Show

Saturday, March 13th, 7:30 P.M.
In the Living Room

Programme:

1) Unfinished Nocturne for Out-of-Tune
Piano and Kazoo
      Composed by Antony Hoffman
       Piano—Antony Hoffman
       Kazoo—Rachel Robinson

2) Richard Bardolis, Magician

3) Winter Fashion Show
      Model—Emily Holly
      Flautist—Janet Hale
    All clothes owned by Emily Holly (not
    for sale)

4) The Doctor's Office, or, Le Bureau du
Médecin
      A bilingual farce by Pierre Cornay
      Le Médecin—Pierre Cornay
      The Patient—Sheila Davis
    Directed by the author

5) "The Care and Feeding of Neurotic Dogs"
    A Lecture by Janet Hale

6) Spontaneous Verse by Martha Duffield
    Guitar background—Sheila Davis

7) Comic Imitations by William Hine

8) Traditional French Folk Songs
      Sung by Sally Green
      Piano—Antony Hoffman

9) Push-Up Competition
      Benjamin Drexler
      Patrick L'Anglais
      Michael Burpee

10) The Last Apple
      A parable in verse by Claudia Thon-
      nard
       Apple—Claudia Thonnard
       Farmer—Michael Fraser
       Worm—Gabrielle Newman
      Costumes by Silvia Pakalns
      Directed by the author

11) "The Silence of Infinity"
      Ballet by Angela Richardson

12) "Animals at the Zoo"—pantomime
      Ann Peacock, George Novotny

13) Folk Songs by Michael Fraser, Banjoist

All Original Material (except Sally's songs)

Dancing and refreshments in the dining room
              afterward

Sheila's new love for Jerry somewhat changed her feelings toward Mimi. They were rivals now, but Sheila preferred to keep her love to herself; so she had to put up with a lot of talk from Mimi, who thought of her as a sympathetic listener.

"I think Jerry and I are really so compatible. I mean, I keep hearing him say things that are *just* the way I feel! He's more conventional than me but not square, he's ma*ture*. And he's tall, and just my type physically. . . . Oh, sometimes I feel we're just *made* for each other! If only *he'd* realize it. . . ."

Sheila's irritation with this sort of thing was making her turn more and more to Sally. Sally was growing a little bored with Ben, but she seldom talked about it. She taught Sheila to play chess. Sheila, though hardly expert, wasn't as bad as Mimi; so now Sally always played with her instead. Now it was Mimi who began to feel left out. With her lack of creative inspiration this term, no Rosalie, no English, no Psychology, her added quarter of an inch in height but none in bulk, and her unrequited love for Jerry, Mimi was rather depressed. She forgot her Resolutions; she left her mice dusty and neglected; she would wander idly around the building or sprawl on her bed, uttering deep sighs.

Janet complained that Mimi wasn't nearly as much fun as she used to be. "Mimi was the liveliest girl in the school, and now she's kind of a drag." She added thoughtfully, "If only Rosalie were here, she could analyze her." But dear, darling, beautiful, brilliant, stimulating Rosalie—now remembered only with love —was gone for good. The Kenners said she wasn't coming back next year. Why not? The Kenners wouldn't say.

One evening, not long before the end of term, Mike came into the library with some interesting news.

"Got a letter from my cousin today—he's at Sedgewick Academy, near Toronto. Anyway, his school and some others are going to get together on the end-of-May long weekend and have a Children's Shakespeare Festival. I mean, each school will do a production of some play by him, and the best will win a prize. They have only three entries so far, and other schools are invited. You have to write and find out what plays are being done and say which you'll do, so there won't be two of the same. They can't have more than six. Let's do something!"

The others found this idea very exciting. Mimi stopped sighing.

Mike and Pierre went to talk to the Kenners. To their surprise and disappointment, neither was at all keen.

"We've never competed with other schools in any way," Kenny said doubtfully.

"Well, why not, this once?" Pierre objected. "You like us to be experimental and try new things."

Willy voiced the objection which was probably the real reason for their lack of enthusiasm.

"Producing a full-length Shakespeare play isn't easy. Neither Kenny nor I feels qualified; we know nothing about dramatic production. And it isn't exactly the kind of thing you students are used to doing on your own, is it? I mean, you always do your own original plays, in your own way. Which is fine—but it's not Shakespeare."

The boys took this to mean that Willy didn't believe they were capable.

"And with all those other schools," Kenny put in, "it's not quite the same as our Saturday entertainments."

They took this to mean that she feared they would make fools of themselves before the other students.

They left the room feeling very indignant.

"Imagine, not thinking us capable! We're *their* students— products of *their* educational system—and they have no confidence in us!"

"They have no *right* to say we can't go; it's undemocratic!

Only their two votes against all the rest of us. It's against the principles of the school!"

"It's not fair!" Mimi cried as she and Sheila joined them, having overheard the indignant conversation. "What're we going to do?"

"We've just *got* to go to that festival!" Sheila exclaimed. "I can't *bear* it if we don't."

"Why, we'll just darn well produce a play of Shakespeare's and show the Kenners we can," said Mike. "Even if Willy won't drive us, we'll get to the festival somehow."

"Yes!" said Mimi eagerly. "I bet we could win, too. Those other creeps will just recite their lines flatly, by rote—they won't be *fresh* and spon*taneous,* like us."

Everybody gathered in the library that evening. The Kenners' lack of enthusiasm made them all the more determined to enter the festival.

"First," said Mike efficiently, "we have to decide on a play. And write to tell them which we're doing, so nobody else can. So far they've got *The Merchant of Venice, Macbeth,* and *Julius Caesar.*"

"Let's do something kind of unusual," Janet suggested, "so we'll get extra credit for being ambitious. What's the play your father was in, Gaby? That one he wouldn't let you see because it was too gory or something."

"*Titus Andronicus.* Oh, I was only six then—he always lets me see his plays now."

"What about that, then?"

"The blood might be tricky if it's really so gory," Pierre said cautiously. "What about *Hamlet?* A lot of us have read it, so it would be easier."

"*Hamlet* has no big women's parts," Mimi protested.

"What about a comedy?" said Sheila, remembering her good

sense of timing. "I bet we could be especially fresh and spontaneous in a comedy."

But the majority felt that *Hamlet,* being familiar, was safest.

Both Mike and Pierre, the most experienced actors among the boys, longed to play Hamlet. An argument now arose over which should have the part. The two boys eyed each other rather coldly and let the others discuss it.

"I think Mike would be best," Sheila decided. "Pierre's just as good an actor, of course, but I think Hamlet should be dark." She herself was hoping for the part of Gertrude, since she felt Ophelia had to be a blonde.

"But he's Danish," Ben protested. "Danes are blond."

"But they're *all* Danish, or Norwegian, or something—and they can't *all* be blonds; we don't have enough to go around."

They decided to vote on it. Mike won by a narrow margin.

"All right," said Pierre resignedly. "But bags I be the king."

"Sure," said Mike, generous now he'd gotten the plum role. "I think you'd be perfect as the king."

The others agreed after a brief argument.

"Now, what about the other parts?"

"Sally for Ophelia," said Dick; again, everybody agreed. Mimi, who thought Gertrude a bore, longed to play romantic Ophelia herself. But she was taller than Mike. All right as his mother, hardly as his sweetheart.

However, neither Sheila nor Mimi got the part of Gertrude. It was generally felt that Janet's plumpness and well-developed bosom were best suited for Hamlet's mother.

The remaining parts were cast, with a good deal of argument, among the other boys. A few girls-as-boys might be needed, as courtiers and so on. Here Mimi's tallness would be an asset; she was thankful, now, to be in the play at all. The girls would also be in charge of costumes, sets, props, and anything else that came up.

The last few days of term were busy with rehearsals.

Mike threw himself into the part of Hamlet with enthusiasm. No longer did he play his banjo or tell sick jokes; he brooded. Finding Stanislavski's *An Actor Prepares* in the library, he studied it, anxious to play the part in true "Method" style. Mike was a lazy reader and did not get very far with the book; but he found a few technical terms which appealed to him. He learned that an actor must first understand the basic motivation of the character he plays—the "verb," it was called. Having felt himself into the character, an actor can then begin to express him outwardly. To begin with the motions, rather than the understanding, was to be "external."

And so, in every waking moment, Mike tried to live the part of Hamlet. He wore black jeans and an old black sweater, and he brooded. Serving himself a generous portion of mashed potatoes, he might sigh deeply and murmur, *"O that this too, too solid flesh would melt . . ."*

At rehearsals Mike was impossible, especially in his dramatic scene with Janet. Here Hamlet was angrily scolding his mother for marrying his wicked uncle soon after the death of his noble father. Janet sat on a chair and Mike stood before her, book in hand (he'd hardly even begun to learn his lines). He frowned darkly at her, then paced around the room, sometimes glancing at the book, sometimes gazing into space. After several minutes of this he stopped, scratched his stomach, and mumbled incoherently: *"An eye like Mars, to threaten and command; A station like the herald Mercury, New-lighted on a heaven-kissing hill . . ."* Then he continued to pace and brood silently.

"Come *on*, Mike," Janet urged. "That speech is thirty-six lines! You'll *never* get through it at this rate."

"Give me time, for heaven's sake. I'm feeling Hamlet's verb."

"But this is the third day we've worked on this scene," George protested, "and we still haven't gotten through it."

Mike glared at him. "You keep out of this. You're dead, I just killed you."

"Yeah—two hours ago!" They had been rehearsing all afternoon.

"Get with it, Mike, will you?" Jerry urged wearily. "I still haven't had a chance to make my entrance." (Jerry was cast as the Ghost, because of his tall slimness.) "I'm getting pretty sick and tired of just hanging around."

Mike continued his speech with a new spurt of vigor. He glared at Janet and spat out his words: *"Ha! have you eyes?*
. . . O shame! where is thy blush?" Janet cringed and clutched at her heart, her bosom heaving with emotion.

Watching, Jerry and George tried not to laugh. They knew she was doing her best, but, oh, dear! She was turning the scene into a grotesque comedy.

Finally it was Janet's cue to speak. She held out a trembling hand and moaned: *"O Hamlet, speak no more: Thou turn'st mine eyes into my very soooul—"*

George burst into a loud guffaw; he couldn't help himself. Janet, hurt, shut up immediately. Mike frowned at her.

"You're too ex*ternal*, Janet. You haven't got her *verb* yet."

She burst into tears. "Oh, for heaven's *sake*. I've been sitting here for hours trying to feel like Gertrude . . . I just can't keep it up! You can get someone *else* to play the part—I *quit!*" Then she jumped up and hurried out of the room.

"Oh, dear," said Mike. "We should've given that part to Sheila."

"It's your own fault," said George. "Poor Janet's worn out

with sitting around while you try and get Hamlet's tiresomely complicated *verb*."

"No, it isn't just that," said Jerry gloomily. "Let's face it, Janet's Gertrude is lousy."

Janet came back and announced very humbly that she would continue the rehearsal. She read her lines a little better this time, but Jerry was beginning to fear *Hamlet* simply was not going to come off. He was as anxious as anybody to get to the festival; but with each rehearsal he lost hope.

The other actors weren't too bad. Pierre as Claudius, the king, had a nice courtly manner; Sally was pretty and appealing as Ophelia. But the production as a whole was not promising. Nobody could really agree on one authoritative director. Pierre tried to direct; but there were too many suggestions, too many arguments. Sally was ready to rewrite the whole play to suit their needs. Janet insisted every line of Shakespeare's was sacred. The usual Kenner way of settling disputes was to vote on them. This method, effective in so many school matters, didn't work well in rehearsals. They dragged on interminably.

Finally even Mike, so absorbed in his part that he noticed little else, couldn't help seeing that the production as a whole was hopeless. But nobody wanted to admit failure. They criticized specific things; nobody had the nerve to suggest *Hamlet* was just too much for them to handle. They had sworn to produce a play for the festival, and the thought of giving up was painful.

A thick cloud of gloom hung over the marshmallow toasters in the library on the last evening of term.

Mike, unbearably restless, paced up and down, humming a gloomy little tune. "Too bad about Louise," he muttered, stopping briefly at Louise's old table, now sadly bare. "This room just isn't the same without her."

A long, glum silence fell. Then Jerry spoke.

"I know how we still might get to the festival. I mean, with *Hamlet,* of course—not just to watch."

"How?"

"Get old Ruthy to direct it."

They stared at him.

"Old *Ruthy?* Are you *crazy?*"

"Oh, I agree it isn't likely he would. If you hadn't all gotten so carried away and gone on strike, he might have. He's directed school productions of Shakespeare plays for years in England. He told me about it one day; he's done tragedies and comedies and everything. He really seems to know a lot about dramatic production—sounds like a real pro."

They all stared at him. Big blond Liz spoke first.

"Oh, you stupid things"—she glared at the English students—"why did you have to go on strike in that silly way? Now you've spoiled everything for *all* of us. He'll never agree to direct *Hamlet* with nearly half the school so impossible."

There were annoyed exclamations from all the other sixteen who weren't taking English.

"It's all right for *you* to talk," Mimi exclaimed indignantly. *"We're* the ones who had him as a teacher! Why *shouldn't* we go on strike?"

"You didn't have to be so *infantile* about it," Liz insisted.

"I guess we could have given old Ruthy a bit more of a chance," Tony said gloomily. "But what was *really* bad was that we went on strike too late. As soon as we found we didn't like his teaching, we should have exercised our privilege not to go to classes and simply dropped English. Then we'd have acted with dignity—instead of still going to classes and grumbling."

"All those silly tricks on Ruthy, like kids at ordinary schools!" said Don scornfully. "Your behavior was un*worthy* of Kenner students."

"I didn't play any tricks," Sally pointed out. "I stopped going

to English after the first week." The others were too subdued to be annoyed by her smugness. They looked at her with grudging respect.

If they had dropped English early in the term, like Sally, Sheila thought gloomily, Mr. Rutherford might have seen them as free people exercising their choice; as things were, he must just think them silly kids who didn't know what they were doing. On the other hand, if they had been nicer to Mr. Rutherford, like Jerry, the teacher might have agreed to direct *Hamlet*. Either extreme would have been all right; but they had chosen an ineffectual middle course.

"Do you think—maybe—there's just a *tiny* chance we might still persuade him to direct the play," she suggested hesitantly. "I mean—if we start off next term *really* well, and go to class and be terribly keen, and good, and study hard."

There was a very, very faint ray of hope.

"Maybe if we're *perfect*," Ben said doubtfully.

"If we go to the first class with those lines written five hundred times . . ."

"A thousand for me," Mimi reminded them.

"Well, let's *all* do them a thousand times, just to be on the safe side. We'll have plenty of time in the holidays."

"Yes," said Janet. "And we girls must always wear skirts to class. The Dirty Look is *out*."

Mimi jumped up, her face alight with inspiration.

"Janet, you've *got* it! Since he doesn't seem to like modern girls, we won't *be* modern—we'll be sweet, feminine, old-fashioned girls! Polite, and prim, and neat, and all that—you must *all* call me Emily."

"Yes! That's *it*, Mimi!"

"And we'll be perfect young gentlemen," Ben said excitedly. "We'll always call him 'sir'—"

"Oh, yes!" said Sally. "And *we'll* be just so sweet and feminine and simpering and prim. . . . Gee, he'll get sick of it, he'll *miss* our Dirty Look, even!"

"Now, don't overdo it," Jerry warned. "We want to please him, remember. Don't make a big production out of it."

"Just be polite," Liz suggested.

But nobody paid any attention to them. The strikers were too carried away by the prospect of being perfect young gentlemen and sweet, feminine, old-fashioned girls. It was going to be fun.

Jerry and his roommates were packing a little later, when Ben appeared in the doorway, grinning.

"Let's give the girls a scare tonight. Let's sneak up on the roof and make noises like ghosts; an old house like this ought to have a ghost or two. We can count on Gaby to scream."

"How *juvenile*," Mike moaned.

"I thought we were supposed to be perfect young gentlemen now," said Jerry.

"Oh, that's next term," Ben insisted. "Tonight doesn't count."

And so the term ended.

Sheila enjoyed the Easter holidays. Snow was melting, in great puddles and rivulets and masses of slush, all over the city; the air was filled with the freshness of spring. She persuaded Mother to buy her some ruffly underwear to take back to school for the Old-Fashioned Look. Of course Mr. Ruthy wouldn't see them; but she would feel more feminine and old-fashioned in them than in her usual plain things.

She still had little clashes with Stan.

"What are you doing still up at this hour?" Stan demanded one night when he and Mother entered the house to find Sheila lying on the living room floor reading a magazine. "It's nearly two o'clock."

Sheila looked up with a scowl. Stan was wearing his dinner

jacket, Mother a beautiful gold brocade gown. "What do *you* care?" she said angrily. "It happens to be the holidays, and I can sleep all day if I want. I'll darn well stay up as late as I like!"

"Sheila," her mother snapped, "I don't want to hear you talking to Stan like that—"

"Wait, Barbara"—Stan put his hand on Mother's arm—"Sheila's right; she *is* on holiday, after all."

"Oh, all right. But be sure and turn out the lights when you *do* go to bed."

Sheila heard their footsteps going upstairs and the murmur of voices. She felt rather flat and left out. Then suddenly she thought of Mimi, Sally, Jerry, and the rest; and all at once Mother and Stan didn't seem to matter so much. She had a life of her own now, apart from them. I guess they have a right to a life of their own too, she decided tolerantly. They're only human, after all. It made her feel very fond of Mother to think of her as only human.

Chapter Eleven

*A*s soon as the new term opened, the English students got ready to please Mr. Rutherford, with their usual enthusiasm for anything new.

"I brought a mechanical mouse to school," Gaby told some of the other girls, unpacking the first evening. "The kind that winds up—very realistic. Anyway, I thought we could get one of the boys to wind it up, and then we girls can jump up on our chairs and scream."

"Oh, Gaby! That's so silly."

"Well, maybe, but we want to show him right away that we're sweet and simpering and old-fashioned, just in case he doesn't get the idea."

The others were scornful, but Gaby was still determined. She accosted Ben downstairs later, when milk and apples were being served in the dining room, and asked him to handle the mouse. To her annoyance, he refused.

"Perfect young gentlemen just don't *do* that kind of thing."

"But how can we show Ruthy we're sweet, feminine, old-fashioned girls if we aren't afraid of mice?"

"How can *we* show him we're perfect young gentlemen if we play such a silly trick on sweet, feminine, old-fashioned girls?"

Gaby had no answer to this.

"Well, I'll have to do it myself," she decided crossly.

"Though I'll look darn silly if old Ruthy sees me wind up the mouse and then jump up on my chair and scream."

Sheila, Mimi, and Sally were undressing when Janet burst into their room, waving a glossy magazine. Her pale eyes shone with excitement.

"Girls—will you just *look* at *this!*"

She opened the magazine at a large, double-page spread.

THE MODERN SCHOOL CHILD

An Analysis of So-Called "Progressive Education"

by Rosalie Dennis

"Gee!" Mimi exclaimed, delighted. "Is that about *us?*"

"It certainly is," said Janet ominously. "We're all in it. She gives us phony names, but it's us—you're 'Lulu,' Mimi. Just *wait till you read it!* It's very insulting. It says how messy we look—and how we don't learn anything, or if we do we're not well-rounded—and how the school is in debt and won't last long because nobody with any sense would contribute money! She says it doesn't prepare us properly for college or jobs or life in the outside world or anything. Listen to *this:* 'I came to teach with an open mind, anxious to see how this free system might benefit its students. I gave it a fair try. There is only one word for this type of education: REgressive.' That's the word the Bartells used, remember?"

There was a long, horrified pause. They were all deeply shocked. Sally spoke first.

"I always *thought* there was something funny about her," she said fiercely. "But I never dreamed she could be so *mean.*"

"Remember that stupid 'boys are better than girls' debate?" Sheila reminded them.

"Oh, yes," said Janet. "She talks about that, too. Something about how we don't have much rivalry between the sexes and this isn't as healthy as it sounds; we're too ambiguous or something. Isn't it awful? I can still hardly believe it. Our own Rosalie!"

Mimi's lip was trembling. Suddenly she collapsed on her bed in a flood of tears.

"Ohhh—how *could* she? I loved her and admired her, and I told her all my neuroses and my dreams and everything, and now . . . she calls me *Lulu!*"

If one more thing had been needed to win them over to Mr. Rutherford, this was it.

Mr. Rutherford entered English class the next morning to find everybody already seated. But they rose politely when he came into the room and said, "Good morning, sir."

He looked at them with interest. The girls all stood in the front row, hands folded, feet together. They wore clean, crisp summer dresses; their hair was smooth and shining. Mimi, eyes cast down demurely, was especially striking. She wore a full-skirted pink dress over several rustling petticoats, with long sleeves and a white lace collar; dainty pink slippers with white bows on the toes; and a big pink bow perched on her reddish hair, which she had twisted into ringlets. Mimi was overdoing it as usual.

The boys were just as neat. Hair slicked down, jackets, ties, newly pressed trousers, and shiny shoes. Mike had had his hair cut again.

Mr. Rutherford surveyed them for a long moment. Then he said casually, "Good morning, class. Please sit down."

Pierre remained standing. "Please, sir," he said, "we've all done those lines you assigned us last term. I'm sorry we took so long. Would you like me to collect them for you, sir?"

"Oh—those lines. All right, Pierre. Collect them and put them in the wastebasket. I hope it won't be necessary for me to give you such a 'pedantic' assignment ever again." A faint ghost of a smile crossed his face. "Open your poetry books at page two fifty-three. Mimi, will you begin reading?"

"Oh—you used to call me Emily."

"Well, it seems everybody else calls you Mimi, so I thought I would too."

"I thought you preferred to call me Emily."

"I'll be perfectly happy to go on calling you Emily if that's what you wish."

"Oh, no," Mimi said hastily. "I mean, call me Mimi if you want. I mean, call me whatever *you* prefer."

"All right, Mimi. Will you begin reading?"

Mimi began in a hushed, breathless voice, and the class proceeded undramatically.

Gaby's trick with her mouse fell very flat. Mimi spoiled it by exclaiming, "Oh, what a cute little mechanical mouse! Where did you get it, Gaby? It's so realistic."

Mr. Rutherford looked at the mouse, said, "Ingenious toy," and put it in his pocket. The class went on without incident.

They left the room feeling vaguely dissatisfied.

"Hey, kids!" Liz and George rushed up to meet the English students. "How did he react? D'you think he's forgiven you for the way you acted last term?"

"I don't know," said Tony, frowning. "He's very calm."

"He's just playing it cool," said Jerry. "But I think he's pleased. And I suspect he knows *why* we decided to reform. He must have heard about us hoping to go to the festival and the Kenners not being keen."

"Oh, dear," said Liz. "Then he must think you're being nice just as a bribe."

"Well, we are," Sheila pointed out.

"Yes, but I hope he doesn't mind too much. It isn't very flattering; his feelings might be hurt or something. Do you think he minds, Jerry?"

"I don't know. I don't think so—I think he's amused, but I can't be sure."

"Maybe he'll offer to do a production of his own accord—if we refer to the festival now and then—tactfully, of course."

"Maybe. Then we'll know he doesn't mind."

They were in too much suspense really to enjoy the annual spring flood—except Pierre, who filmed it. Melting ice and snow, rushing down the mountain, had swelled the river until it rose over the playing field, carrying interesting bits of floating debris: old tires, a baby carriage, barrels, a screen door, part of a chicken coop with a bedraggled hen perched miserably on top. One of the boys took out a rowboat and rescued the hen, which became a favorite pet. She wandered around the school building clucking cheerfully, and laid eggs in unexpected places. They named her Alice.

Sheila had always longed to be in a flood. The idea of having to move upstairs or on the roof, to sail down streets in a boat, half-submerged buildings rising on either side; this had always thrilled her—even the simple sight of trees rising out of murky gray water. Unfortunately the school buildings, perched high above the river, were many feet out of danger.

But the festival was only six weeks away . . . five weeks . . . a little more than four weeks. A few guarded references were made to it at mealtimes, in Mr. Rutherford's hearing. Surely he must know about their attempts to produce *Hamlet* on their own! The rehearsals hadn't exactly been secret; he must *know!* They got into the habit, whenever passing him in the hallways, of saying, "Hello, sir," and gazing at him very wistfully. But still he said nothing.

The suspense was unbearable. Trooping into class one morning, his English students all gave him a particularly appealing look. But he seemed not to notice it.

"Open your poetry anthologies at page eighty-four," he said calmly. "Gaby will begin reading."

Sheila caught Mike's eye. They exchanged a long, gloomy look and, at that moment, lost all hope. There would be no play: that was that.

Gaby opened her book and cleared her throat to read. Suddenly she could bear it no longer. She cried out: "Oh, Mr. Rutherford, aren't you going to direct our play for the festival?"

Everybody started. Gaby turned bright red and burst into tears. "Oh, I'm sorry, I'm sorry, I shouldn't have said it—forget it, sir. Just pretend I never . . ." Her voice trailed away, for Mr. Rutherford was suddenly smiling.

"At *last!*" He let out a deep sigh of relief. "I was wondering when one of you would finally get around to asking me. We've only four more weeks to rehearse, you know. Thank heavens you finally spoke up before it was too late, Gaby!"

"Then—you *want* to do it, sir?"

"Of course I do! I've got the whole production planned in my mind—I worked it all out in the holidays."

"But, then—why didn't *you* speak to *us?*"

Mr. Rutherford smiled his nice, quietly humorous smile.

"Well, Gaby, somehow I preferred to wait and let you children come to me. I felt I deserved it."

Everybody laughed, delighted and relieved. Mr. Rutherford's laughter joined theirs. But then he became businesslike.

"You can tell the other students that auditions will begin after lunch tomorrow. I hope everybody in the school will come to read. Especially the boys. I'll need every boy I can get."

"But, sir, it's already been cast," Dick protested. "Unless you'd prefer Pierre as Hamlet—"

"Oh, I've no intention of doing *Hamlet* with you children;

robust comedy is more in your line. We'll be doing *The Taming of the Shrew*. I've already got the Kenners' permission and notified the festival. As soon as it's cast, we'll get to work: and I expect *hard* work, mind you—long, grueling rehearsals, afternoon *and* evening. I hope you're all prepared for this."

Mike was not too pleased at losing Hamlet; but the others were delighted. If any production by Kenner students was likely to be comic, why not start with a comedy in the first place?

"Oh, one more thing," Mr. Rutherford added, and they all looked at him expectantly. "If you think my decision to produce the play changes anything, you're mistaken. What I mean to say is, I expect your model behavior in English class to continue."

"You mean—even our clothes?" Jerry asked. "Ties and slicked hair and everything?"

"I do. I've enjoyed your performance as perfect young gentlemen and sweet, feminine, old-fashioned girls so much I'd like to go on being entertained for the rest of the term."

He smiled rather impishly. Jerry smiled back with rueful admiration. Yes, you had to hand it to old Ruthy: the guy was really cool.

At lunch Willy made an announcement. He was smiling as he entered the room.

"I have an exciting piece of news, which probably most of you have heard about from the English students; but in case you haven't, here it is. Nicholas Rutherford is going to direct a production of *The Taming of the Shrew*, which we will take to the new Children's Shakespeare Festival at Sedgewick, Ontario, the last weekend in May. Even for those of you who don't get parts, I'm sure the festival will be fun." ("*Now* he thinks it'll be fun," Mike muttered crossly to Pierre, who smiled back ruefully.)

"Readings will take place tomorrow at two P.M. in the living room," Kenny added. She was smiling too. "I hope everybody will show up."

"Especially the boys," Mr. Rutherford put in from the back of the room. "Not too many girls' parts in *Taming of the Shrew*, I'm afraid."

That evening everybody was full of excitement over tomorrow's audition. Mimi had never read *The Taming of the Shrew*, but she knew *Kiss Me, Kate* and talked happily about the two heroines as she and her roommates got ready for bed. "They're sisters, Kate and Bianca—the same name as Kenny's," she marveled, "but an utterly different type. Kate is wild and rebellious till she marries a man called Petruchio, who tames her. Bianca's quiet and feminine and obedient, but a bit of a minx too. Gee, Mr. Ruthy just couldn't have picked a better play—the parts are simply *made* for Sally and me!" She added kindly, "Too bad there's no part quite right for you, Sheila. Anyway, you'll still be going to the festival. Oh, it's going to be a *gas*."

Sheila said nothing, but she was secretly anxious to get the part of Kate. She had been in the library all afternoon, reading the play and thinking about its heroine. She wasn't sure she liked her. Kate was lively, all right; but *such* a shrew. Rude to her father, mean to her sister, impossible to her tutors—she hit her music master over the head with a lute. On the other hand, most of the other characters were a bit hard on Kate. Her father seemed to have always preferred her younger sister, and naturally Kate resented this. Sheila didn't like her very much—she found the dashing, funny Petruchio more appealing—but she felt she understood her.

All thirty-two students came to the readings in the living room. Mike, having lost Hamlet, was hoping for Petruchio. But the part was promptly given to Tony.

"Type casting," Mike muttered disgustedly. He was consoled

by getting the part of Gremio, a rich old man, one of Bianca's many suitors.

Mimi was delighted with Tony as Petruchio. He was an inch and a half taller than herself; they would make a perfect pair.

"You're next, Mimi."

Suddenly she was terrified. Her legs shook; her hands trembled. To look more like Kate, she had stuffed her brand-new bra with Kleenex. But she didn't feel at all like Kate, more like a very tall mouse. Sheila watched her go up to Mr. Rutherford somewhat unsteadily.

"Take your time, Mimi," he said kindly. "I want to see each of you girls do your best before I cast the women's parts."

Mimi's voice was wobbly at first, but soon grew more confident. She read one of Kate's wilder scenes; Mr. Rutherford read the other parts. Watching, Sheila couldn't help feeling that Mimi's Kate was far too frivolous, not enough of a real shrew. She also read a scene of Bianca's and a final speech of Kate's, when she has finally been tamed into an obedient, submissive wife: *"I am ashamed that women are so simple To offer war where they should kneel for peace . . ."* Mr. Rutherford asked her to read part of the speech over again. Sheila noticed that he was asking all the girls to reread that particular one.

"Thank you, Mimi. Sheila next."

Mimi retired to the other end of the room feeling she hadn't done too badly. The competition wasn't very impressive. Liz was energetic but too bouncy. Rachel was a Bianca type. Janet was better, although a bit dumpy-looking. She had read the part with great vigor and charm: exuberant in the fighting scenes, soft and womanly in the final one.

Sheila was standing ready now. She looked very still and composed. And awfully un-Kate-like in her blue blouse and skirt: childish, and not very attractive. But then she started to read, and she changed. She came alive, looked taller and older somehow, and her dark eyes flashed sparks. Her voice had harsh notes in it which Janet's hadn't; she was a less appealing Kate but more interesting. There was no doubt about it: Sheila was good. But when she read the submissive speech, it sounded a little bit harsh too. Not soft like Janet, who had read it so perfectly.

"The first few lines again, Sheila," Mr. Rutherford said.

Sheila read again.

"How do you see Kate here, Sheila? What d'you think she's feeling?"

Sheila hesitated a moment, struggling to put it into words. "Well, her speech is completely obedient and submissive, like she's really given in. But she's so wild through most of the play, I can't believe she's changed so much as all that. I mean, she's resigned, and I guess she *will* be an obedient wife from now on—but she's proud, too. I mean, I think the whole speech is a bit sarcastic—just a *bit*, though. She's resigned, but she isn't completely happy about it. It just seems the best thing to do."

"I see, Sheila; that's an interesting interpretation. Thank you. Sally next."

Sheila left feeling rather dissatisfied. Somehow she hadn't done her best. She hadn't gotten exactly the right quality into that speech. It had to be subtle: it shouldn't sound sarcastic to Petruchio, only to the audience.

She joined Mimi on the sofa. Mimi looked suspicious.

"Where did you get all these theories about Kate's personality?"

"Theories? Well, I was just reading the play and—"

"*Oh*—you read the *play*." She cheated, Mimi thought sulkily; oh, gee, why hadn't she thought to read the play herself?"

Sally gave quite a spirited reading.

"Very nice," said Mr. Rutherford. "Well, that's all the girls, isn't it? All right, then: Sheila is Kate, Sally is Bianca . . ."

Oh, *why* didn't I bother to read the play? Mimi moaned inwardly. And then she wondered if it would have made any difference. One thing she was pretty sure of by now: Sheila had talent. Sheila was in a different class from herself on stage; all of a sudden Mimi knew this. How *could* she have been so stupid as to imagine Sheila wasn't right for Kate? Though I still like Janet's Kate better, she thought sulkily.

Jerry was congratulating Sheila and Sally on their success. The three stood chatting animatedly; Sheila's eyes were shining. She really is kind of striking, Mimi thought gloomily. The Old-Fashioned Look, so cute on Sally, didn't really do much for Sheila; but during the Dirty Look period she really had been kind of attractive—interesting, anyway. Maybe Jerry found her frequently sullen, brooding look mysterious? Mimi felt lower and lower. If she didn't force herself to get up soon and congratulate the girls, it was going to be harder and harder to do. . . .

Mr. Rutherford joined the cheerful trio.

"What's the matter, Jerry? You seem to be the only person who hasn't read yet."

"Must I, sir? I'm not keen on acting. Can't you just fill me in as a walk-on?"

"Tell you what, then—you needn't be on stage at all. We're going to have to use a few girls-as-boys in walk-on parts anyway; rather a surplus of them around. Your job will be to make the sets."

"Make the sets!"

"I'll give you a floor plan and any instructions you need."

"But I've never *made* sets!"

"Pierre and I will design them. Your job is just to make them."

"But I've never—"

"Well, why not start now? Rehearsal at two tomorrow, girls. And start learning your lines. Sheila, I like your interpretation of Kate." He smiled and hurried away.

"How can I?" Jerry complained. "I won't have time, I've got so many courses."

"Well," said Sheila, "the Kenners don't mind us neglecting subjects when we're caught up and involved in something we're keen on."

"But I'm *not* keen!"

"Well, *get* keen, then," Sally suggested, smiling impishly.

He laughed. "Guess I'll have to, won't I?"

Mimi came running over.

"Congratu*lations,* you two! Gee, I'm proud to have such talented roommates! You'll be *perfect* as Kate and Bianca—a wonderful contrast! I was afraid for a moment Janet would get Kate; but luckily Ruthy realized Sheila's interpretation is far more interesting."

The other two girls, knowing how much she had wanted Kate, were touched by the generosity of her enthusiasm.

It was an unusually warm May—like summer already. The playing field dried up; the sun was hot. Willy, in one of the sudden inspirations which so endeared him to his students, started a class in marine biology. It was a rather specialized branch, limited to life in the river, mainly leeches. The pupils, dressed in bathing suits and goggles, armed with long hollow reeds for breathing, made brief excursions under water to view the fish and frogs. In spite of the coldness of the water, it was quite a popular course. They caught some frogs and put them in a pail with a lid, alive, to dissect in the lab; but Gaby found them and set them free.

The English students, all fifteen of them, went to class in their old-fashioned dresses and neat suits every day. But after a week, Dick accosted Mr. Rutherford boldly one morning at breakfast.

"Sir, I've decided I'd really rather not take English this term. I'm not interested in Jane Austen or Wordsworth."

"What about your promise to humor me because of the play?"

"Well, you're already directing it; you wouldn't stop *now*, would you?" Dick grinned. "D'you want me to keep coming to English just as a bribe? I'm no asset to the class."

"I'll agree with you on *that* point!" Mr. Rutherford's eyes twinkled. "Well, it's up to you. But if you do quit, I can't have you changing your mind. It upsets the class when people keep dropping out and then coming back."

"Oh, of course; I won't come back. It's nothing personal, sir. I just can't stand Jane Austen."

Soon Mike, Sally, Patrick, Bill, Jack, Janet, and Gaby followed Dick's example. The remaining seven, however, were rather liking Mr. Rutherford's class.

"I can't be*lieve* it!" Mimi exclaimed. "All of a sudden it doesn't seem to matter so much that Mr. Ruthy teaches differently from Rosalie. Why did we make such a fuss? He's really a nice old thing. And gee, sometimes reciting poetry can be kind of fun."

"I know," said Sheila. "It's a bit like acting."

But everybody's interest was concentrated on *The Taming of the Shrew*. Even students with no parts in the play and students who found Shakespeare a bore were excited by the festival itself. They had never played sports against other schools; they had lived in their own self-contained little world. Now they found themselves excited by the prospect of coming out of that world for one weekend, of meeting other students as a school.

Mr. Rutherford was the most excited of all. No longer was he "cool"; he was a whirlwind of energy. Seven days a week, in every spare moment, he rehearsed his actors mercilessly.

Rehearsals of the whole cast or big groups were held every afternoon, and these were the most wearisome. Mr. Rutherford found this cast of sixteen individualists, each with his or her own interpretation of the play, sometimes difficult to merge into one complete whole. Mike was especially argumentative. He felt Mr. Rutherford's direction was far too "external."

"How can you just *tell* me to go stage left and then stand facing right?" he exclaimed. "I'm not at all sure Gremio *would* move left at this point."

"Which way *do* you think he'd move?"

"I'm not sure. . . . He might not move at all. I can't be sure of anything yet; I've only just begun to feel my way into his character. Maybe in a couple of weeks I'll get his verb."

"Well, I suggest that instead of waiting two weeks and wasting our precious time, you solve the whole question very simply by accepting my direction, and *move left immediately*."

"But that isn't the Method," Mike objected.

"It's *my* method."

Pierre argued more politely than Mike. He had been cast as Lucentio, another of Bianca's suitors, whom she finally marries. Pierre felt Ruthy's concept of Lucentio was too boringly "straight"—that he wasn't being allowed to exploit all the comic possibilities of the role.

"Lucentio's not a fool, for heaven's sake," Mr. Rutherford said impatiently. "He's primarily romantic; he marries her, remember?"

172

"Then the more fool he, since by the end of the play she's already showing signs of turning into a shrewish wife."

Mr. Rutherford laughed.

"You're right, Pierre; he *is* rather a fool not to see through her earlier. All right, but don't ham it."

"It's not a question of ham. It's a matter of combining a romantic and a comic quality all in one: that's Lucentio as I see him."

"Good, good"—Mr. Rutherford looked at him with new respect—"if you can get that rather delicate balance."

"I can try," said Pierre modestly.

Sally, at least, was no problem. Her Bianca was sweet, lightly comic, rather a minx. She and Pierre made a delightful pair.

In the evenings Mr. Rutherford worked with individuals or small groups. Often he rehearsed Sheila and Tony in the stable after dinner. Under his expert direction Sheila found herself gaining new power as an actress. She was learning how to use her voice as an instrument, just as she did in singing class. Her singing lessons had certainly helped: Sheila had learned to breathe so that even a whisper would reach the back row of the audience. Tony, who had never been considered one of the "school actors," was a delightful Petruchio. He was comic, but also subtle. He tamed Kate with cleverness, not roughness; there was no spanking scene. And he was all the funnier because of it.

Every day at dinner, bolting her food before the evening's rehearsal, Sheila observed Rachel's increasingly cold glances in her direction.

"Haven't noticed you in the library much lately," Rachel commented once, her pretty gray eyes narrowed with suspicion. Rachel was still library officer. "Lost your interest in literature?"

"Oh, I'm too busy rehearsing with Tony and Mr. Ruthy."

Sheila suddenly understood the reason for Rachel's coldness: Tony was officially Rachel's steady boyfriend. They danced together at all the Saturday dances, and Rachel was knitting him some socks. She carried her knitting everywhere, even to class. How silly of her to be jealous! Sheila was still in love with Jerry, in spite of her absorption with herself as Kate. In her few spare moments she helped him with the set-building in the stable loft. She wasn't too handy with a hammer, but he was glad to have her paint things. When he smiled, approving her work, she glowed happily.

The evenings were lengthening. When Mr. Rutherford, Sheila, and Tony finished a rehearsal in the stable, they might find the sky still light. The air was warm, filled with the scent of new grass and wild flowers. The front lawn, totally neglected, was an exotic wilderness of long grass, clover, and dandelions. Sometimes, if they finished a rehearsal early, the three of them would stroll by the river, talking excitedly about the play; and occasionally they took out one of the rowboats. Mr. Rutherford and Tony rowed while Sheila bailed. And they would continue to discuss *The Taming of the Shrew*.

"I wonder if Kate will make a good mother when she has her child?" Sheila might remark.

"I bet Petruchio will make a good father," Tony would add.

"Certainly," Mr. Rutherford would put in, "things will never be dull in *that* household!" And they would talk about how many children Kate and Petruchio might have, what names they would give them, and so on.

All the boys in the school, except Jerry, had parts in the play, but very few of the girls. Besides Kate and Bianca the only other woman's part was that of a widow. Liz, Mimi, and three others had been cast as minor manservants. But even the girls with no parts at all were very busy. Afternoon and evening they would gather in the art studio with Cokes and transistor radios, and gossip and busily sew costumes. Mr. Rutherford had suggested simplified versions of Renaissance styles, bold and bright, well suited to the spirit of the play. Several girls had gone to Beloeil, the town across the river, and bought yards and yards of bright material.

"How are you girls getting on with the costumes?" Kenny asked Liz in the chemistry lab one morning. Through the wall came the sounds of hammering from the carpentry workshop, where some boys were building a new canoe. "Need any help?"

"Oh, yes! We've only that one sewing machine and it doesn't work too well. A lot has to be done by hand. We need every helper we can get."

So in the evenings Kenny joined the costume crew. So did Jeanne, Mildred, and Madame. Even Willy dropped in occasionally; he was good at making hats.

"Thank goodness!" Sally exclaimed one day, coming into the art studio, where a dozen girls sat sewing capes. "I finally broke up with Ben, just now. We decided it was the best thing for both of us." Sally looked radiant. She was even prettier since she had turned thirteen.

Mimi frowned at her across a wide expanse of purple cloth. You might think she'd just fallen in love, not broken up with an old boyfriend, Mimi thought irritably. She was a bit annoyed with Sally these days. Sally—who often danced with Jerry at the Saturday dances—didn't deserve to be so popular with boys. She was so cool: she didn't *need* love, and had so little to offer. It wasn't fair. As for Mimi herself—oh, she just *knew* she was unusually passionate! Friends who thought her lighthearted simply had no idea how much love she had to give. If only Jerry—or somebody as great as he—would come along and find out!

The girls worked hard at the costumes. But sometimes after dinner it was impossible to remain indoors. The warm air and pungent smells were stimulating. They made some students prone to mischief and put others in the mood for romance. Girls escaped into the garden to meet boyfriends, to exchange kisses, and go boating until sunset. Often Mimi, filled with unbearable restlessness, would escape herself; but she had no boyfriend to meet. She would stroll by the river, alone, sighing deeply, heart filled with longing under her Kleenex-stuffed bra. She had had her first date at eleven; she had been to many dances; she had kissed; she had necked; but she still hadn't had a real romance. And she would be fourteen in August!

One evening toward the middle of May, Mr. Rutherford was again rehearsing Sheila and Tony in the stable. They were having trouble with the witty scene between Kate and Petruchio when they first meet.

Petruchio has heard of Kate's reputation as a shrew. She is a challenge to him; he is determined to woo her, wed her, and tame her. His greeting is comically gallant:

> PETRUCHIO. Hearing thy mildness praised in every town,
> Thy virtues spoke of, and thy beauty sounded,
> Yet not so deeply as to thee belongs,
> Myself am moved to woo thee for my wife.

> KATE. Moved? In good time: let him that moved you hither
> Remove you hence. I knew you at the first,
> You were a movable.

> PETRUCHIO. Why, what's a movable?

> KATE. A joint-stool.

> PETRUCHIO. Thou hast hit it: come sit on me. . . .

Here Tony would sit down on a bench and pat his leg invitingly. Sheila would toss her head and turn away, flinging back over her shoulder, scornfully: " 'Asses are made to bear, and so are you.' "

Many lines of witty point and counterpoint followed. It was an important scene but, so far, not successful. The witty lines flung back and forth grew rather monotonous.

"You must show Petruchio's cleverness here," Mr. Rutherford told Tony. "This is the beginning of his campaign to tame Kate. Wit isn't enough; it must have great spirit and determination."

A little wearily they continued.

" 'I knew you at the first,' " snapped Sheila. " 'You were a movable.' "

" 'Why, what's a movable?' "

" 'A joint-stool'—Oh!"

She gave a startled little gasp as Tony grabbed her from behind and bounced her on his knee. Grinning widely, he said: " 'Thou hast it: come, sit on me.' "

And Sheila, quickly recovering her composure, replied tartly: " 'Asses are made to bear, and so are you.' "

Mr. Rutherford chuckled delightedly. "Tony, that's *it!*—you must play it like that. Sheila, your startled expression and then your recovery are very funny—try doing it again."

They went through the whole scene twice. They didn't need Mr. Rutherford to tell them that now the scene worked. They could feel it; the scene was alive.

Mr. Rutherford ended the rehearsal early because it had gone so well. "You know," he remarked thoughtfully as the three left the stable, "I'm beginning to see a few virtues in you children— all of you, I mean. You really do have a great deal of individual insight into the characters you play. This alone isn't enough; it takes one recognized authority to produce a dramatic perfor- mance with a large cast. But your individual qualities are important too. Well, at last the play is really beginning to take shape!"

It was an especially beautiful evening, warm and dreamy.

"Let's take a boat out, Mr. Ruthy," Tony suggested. They had all stopped calling him "sir," but he didn't seem to mind.

Mr. Rutherford liked the idea. They selected the least leaky one; Tony pushed it away from the shore, then jumped in with the others. They noticed the new canoe was missing.

"I hope a good swimmer took it," said Mr. Rutherford, not too anxiously, as he was so preoccupied by the play.

"Remember that time Phil took out the old canoe, before we'd even met him?" Tony said to Sheila. Mr. Rutherford, of course, had heard all about Phil. "I wonder how he is now."

"I don't know," said Sheila; but she did know something. Yesterday, while she had helped him paint, Jerry had shown her a letter he had unexpectedly received from Phil. It had startled, touched, and rather embarrassed him. It was very brief:

Dear Jerry,

I have moved to Toronto, to live with some relatives. My psychiatrist just moved too. I hear that Kenner School is going to put on *The Taming of the Shrew* in the festival at Sedgewick at the end of the month. I am not going to school now, but I have private lessons.

If anybody asks you about me, you can say I am better. I am depressed, but my psychiatrist says this is normal and just a stage.

I don't quite know why I am writing you. It was hearing about your play that made me want to. Please don't bother writing back. I just wanted to say I am all right. Good luck in the festival.

Yours Sincerely,

Phil ("The Pill") Bruce

"Oh, dear—he knows that nickname," Sheila exclaimed.

"Sure, everybody finds out their secret nicknames." Jerry frowned down at the letter. "I must write him back, of course. But I'm not sure what to say. I don't want to embarrass him."

"Why don't you tell him about our work on the play? He sounds interested. Oh, and ask him to come and see it, since he lives in Toronto and it's nearby."

"Good idea; I'll do that."

He hadn't asked Sheila to keep the letter a secret or anything. But she did so. She liked to think of it as a confidence. It was the only really encouraging sign that he cared for her. As a friend, anyway. As a girl? She didn't know.

Tony rowed the boat; Mr. Rutherford talked about the play. For once Sheila was only half listening. Her face had a dark, brooding look; Tony thought she looked sullen. But she was feeling dreamy. The beauty of the river in the twilight filled her with vague longings. She had never felt like this before. If only Jerry were here! She almost resented Tony and Mr. Ruthy for not being him. But even without Jerry, life seemed full of endless wonderful possibilities. She was really more happy than sad.

"Hey," said Tony suddenly, "there's Mimi, in the canoe!"

They saw her some distance ahead, drifting near shore. Mimi, picturesque in blue organdy, half reclined in the canoe, her hair drooping in her face. One hand, over the side, languidly trailed a blue ribbon in the water. As they neared they heard her singing plaintively to herself:

> Sing willow, willow, willow, willow,
> Sing willow, willow, willow, *wil*-low,
>   Must be my gar-land. . . .

"Mimi!" Mr. Rutherford called sternly. "Did you pass the swimming test? Where's your paddle?"

Mimi looked around and blushed darkly. Her face was so pink, the smears of Clearasil on her chin stood out palely.

"Oh—the paddle," she said vaguely, composing herself. "I don't want a paddle; what use is it? I have nowhere to go. . . . I only want to drift, endlessly, give myself to the river . . . wherever it wants to take me. . . ."

"Mimi, you didn't even *take* the swimming test," Tony reminded her.

Mimi suddenly discovered the paddle in the bottom of the canoe; she was sitting on it. Mr. Rutherford insisted on sternly following her back to the dock. When she got out, he decided to go ashore too, and escorted her back to school, lecturing sternly while she gradually grew less languid and more sulky. The other two remained sitting in the boat, reluctant to go indoors.

A string of weathered gray barges drifted slowly by, silent and smooth. The sun was setting, the sky pink and orange and green behind smoky, gray-blue wisps of cloud. Sheila ached with longing. If only Jerry were there! Suddenly, and very purposefully, Tony leaned forward and kissed her. Startled, she quickly recovered herself and closed her eyes. It was a long kiss. She was just beginning to enjoy it when he moved away.

Sheila opened her eyes. His face was still close to hers. His eyes were as dark as her own, not gray-blue like Jerry's; his lashes were long, his lips thin.

He smiled, then leaned forward to kiss her again. She closed her eyes expectantly. . . .

"Tony!" a high voice called loudly. "Where are you?"

Tony jumped up, and Sheila opened her eyes. "That's Rachel," he said hastily. "I better go see her. Tie the boat up, will you?" He hurried away.

Sheila sat in the boat awhile longer to savor the moment. She was a little bothered about it but not much. How could she enjoy kissing Tony when she was in love with Jerry? Was she maybe not really in love with him after all? But she knew she was—as much as ever. The kiss made no difference. If only it *had* been Jerry! Still, it was her first kiss, and it was precious. When she closed her eyes, she could still feel it. She vowed not to wash her face for at least a week. A pity the Dirty Look was Out this term.

She returned to her room feeling dreamy, as though living in a different, more exciting dimension than Mimi and Sally. Mimi—curled on her bed, blue organdy crushed—was rather sulkily playing with her mice. Sally was frowning at her fish. "He doesn't look too well," she said. "I hope he won't die like the other."

Sheila eyed them with condescending pity. Poor Mimi, still so childish in spite of her age, playing with toys! And Sally, all worked up about a fish! While Sheila was full of the worldly knowledge that you could be sincerely in love with one boy and still enjoy kissing another. She felt very mature.

Rachel was colder than ever to Sheila after that. To her surprise, so was Tony. He seemed anxious to avoid her. Why? Boys were certainly strange. But she really didn't care much, since he wasn't Jerry. How silly he was!

"Jerry's set is really great," she told Mimi happily as they got ready for bed after another busy day. "It looks really professional."

Mimi, her eyes watery, was scanning the line of pill bottles along the mantelpiece. "There seems to be some new kind of pollen this spring," she mumbled stuffily. "I've tried just about every pill I've got, and nothing works."

"The set will be finished in a few days," Sheila went on, bored with Mimi's allergies. She climbed into bed and rested her head gingerly on the pillow, anxious not to disturb her careful arrangement of curlers. Lately she had been obsessed by her hair. She took nearly an hour with the pink plastic rollers, and they were awfully uncomfortable to sleep on; but it was worth it.

Suddenly Mimi turned to look at her. Through a watery film, her red-brown eyes were shrewd.

"Sometimes, when I hear you go on about Jerry and that precious set, I begin to wonder if *you* have a crush on him too."

"Oh, I adore him *madly!*" Sheila clutched her heart and rolled her eyes wildly. "I'm so jealous of every girl he even *looks* at I could *murder* them." (At least, she was thinking triumphantly, he didn't let Mimi help him with the set when she offered; she's too awkward.)

"Many a great truth is spoken in jest," Mimi snapped back. But she seemed to be only joking. All the same, Sheila had better watch herself. Maybe it would be wise to be less friendly with Mimi. These days, Sheila liked Sally better. They were together often, rehearsing Kate and Bianca's scenes in the afternoons; they acted well together. Sally was really more her friend than Mimi now.

And Jerry worked on the set—with a bit of help from Sheila. The pieces had to be easily movable by bus; but they could be lashed firmly to the ski rack on top. Mr. Rutherford had talked Pierre out of his original design: a picturesque setting of high walls, a grape arbor, and half a house. He finally evolved a simpler idea: two archways, connected by a wall; stylized trees bearing golden fruit; and a gold screen. It could suggest outdoors or indoors, with a few tables and benches added or removed by the girls-as-menservants.

A simple design; but Jerry didn't find the pieces easy to

make. The archways, delicately curved, were built upon a framework of thin boards, then covered with canvas and painted. Jerry spent most of his spare time in the loft, his nostrils filled with the scent of paint and sawdust. When the first archway collapsed, he grumbled. When the second wouldn't stand up, he fumed. But he went on working, hot and sweaty in the airless loft. Hours sped by, unbelievably fast. And there was still so much to do!

For the first time all year he began cutting classes frequently.

"Mon Dieu Seigneur!" Ian exclaimed when Jerry entered the French classroom after four days' absence. *"C'est* Gerald Dressler, *vraiment!* So you've decided to honor us with your presence today?"

"Why *shouldn't* I cut classes?" said Jerry angrily. "I *thought* this school was supposed to be so *free* and all. *On peut dire que c'est une specialité de la maison ici—hein,* Jeanne? *Toujours le liberté!"*

"La *liberté,"* Jeanne said impatiently.

"But if you get too far behind," Ian went on, "you'll hold the rest of the class back. We've just about finished *Les Insolences."*

"It's all very well for *you* to talk!" Jerry exclaimed. *"You* don't have to build that lousy set! I have exactly nine days to finish."

"Well, I have to rehearse! And I still make it to class."

"If you're simply too busy to keep up with French class," Rachel put in gently, "why not just drop the course for the rest of the term?"

"I don't *feel* like dropping it," said Jerry sulkily. "My French will get rusty."

"Then try not to miss class *too* often, Jerry, okay?" Jeanne suggested. *"Eh bien. Expliques-toi, en français, comment tu fais cette mise-en-scène. . . ."*

Finally everything was finished—just in time for a dress rehearsal in the living room. Costumes were still pinned here and there; the paint on the wall was still wet . . . and Mike *would* have to go and lean against it. But everything was done. The archways rose to either side, dull purple, connected by a pale green wall. Sticking up over the wall were flat cut-out trees with olive-green leaves and golden apples ("Apples even in the *play*," Gaby complained). It looked very Renaissance and set off the costumes beautifully: green and gold, blue and yellow, purple and gray.

"Boy, that set is really neat," Ben exclaimed. Jerry felt a burst of happy pride.

After the dress rehearsal (which went very badly) Jerry found a letter from home in his mailbox:

> Dear Jer,
>
> I only wish we could fly up to see your play, but you know how busy we both are finishing this research project.
>
> How are you enjoying the school this term? You spoke of it as slightingly as ever last vacation; but your letters somehow give the impression you're having a very good time.
>
> Jer, we'd love to have you home next year, going to the local High School. But we also feel Kenner's probably doing you more good than you realize. So if you want to stay on another year we'll be happy to finance it. It's up to you entirely.
>
> Best of luck in the Festival.
>
> > Love,
> > > Dad
>
> P.S. Please take a color photograph of your set, honey, so we can see it. I'm proud of you.
> > > Love, Mom

Jerry scowled irritably. Why bring up this choice about next year, for heaven's sake? They *knew* he wanted to go to the high school. Why question him when it was already settled? Maybe it's because they're psychologists, he thought disgustedly. It really wasn't fair that he should be burdened with parents who were *both* psychologists.

Chapter Twelve

Several hundred copies of the programs had been printed. The sets were fastened to the top of the bus; the boxes of costumes were packed inside.

They would leave promptly after an early breakfast Friday morning, and arrive at Sedgewick Academy, host to the festival, in time for dinner. They had been invited to eat at the school. Small groups of two to four students would board at various houses in the town of Sedgewick; the Kenners, Mr. Rutherford, Jeanne, and Mildred were to stay at the academy itself. The other schools taking part in the festival, being located in or around Toronto, would just drive out for performances.

Everybody was very excited.

The Sedgewick boys were extremely curious to meet the students from Kenner. The old story about a Kenner kid shooting a teacher had been resurrected with embellishments. And somehow Phil's setting fire to the stable had gotten around—greatly exaggerated, of course: he had burned the school building to the ground, and students and teachers were living in the stable. The masters were politely prepared to be good hosts; the boys were eager to be entertained by a bunch of nuts.

When the shabby old bus (looking no better since Willy had partially repainted it a different shade of green) stopped outside the imposing, slightly prisonlike gray building, every Sedgewick boy was either out in front or glued to a window. Over two hundred pairs of eyes saw the group of boys and girls who emerged, rather stiff and weary after the long drive.

And what a sad disappointment! Fourteen boys, a little travel-rumpled but if anything neater than Sedgewick at its most formal: short hair, suits, clean shirts, ties, shiny shoes. The eighteen girls, whom they had expected to be either tomboys or beatniks, were even more disappointing. Flowery summer dresses with full skirts, nylons, even hair ribbons. One of them (Mimi, in a ruffly pinafore over a blouse with huge puffed sleeves) could have come straight out of *Little Women*.

They saw Dr. Marston, their headmaster, and Mrs. Marston come out and greet the visitors, who all shook hands politely. The smallest girl (Gaby) even curtsied; and one boy (Pierre) gave Mrs. Marston a gallant little bow.

A bell rang. Dr. and Mrs. Marston led the visitors into the dining hall, a huge, spare, utilitarian room. Founders' portraits glared down forbiddingly from the walls. The boys filed in, curious in spite of their disappointment. Dr. Marston said grace; they began to eat.

Food was one of Sedgewick's economies, not its virtues; but tonight, to please the guests, the kitchen produced fifteen fragrant, flaky apple pies for dessert. The boys were delighted; but they noticed the guests eating theirs politely, without great enthusiasm.

After dinner Dr. Marston said that, as the visitors must be tired, they had better be allowed to go straight to their various accommodations. Tomorrow, after the first play, the schools could meet socially.

Matt Barlow, one of the day boys, was enjoying his prestige as host to four of the girls for the weekend: Sheila Davis, Mimi

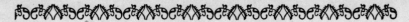

SEDGEWICK CHILDREN'S SHAKESPEARE FESTIVAL

Sponsored by Sedgewick Academy, Sedgewick, Ontario
SEDGEWICK AUDITORIUM, SUNDAY, 8:00 P.M.

Programme:
Kenner School Presents

THE TAMING OF THE SHREW

Cast:

Baptista Minola, father to Kate
    and Bianca .... *George Novotny*
Vincentio, father to Lucentio .... *Jack Victor*
Gremio, a pantaloon, suitor to
    Bianca .... *Michael Fraser*
Lucentio, in love with Bianca,
    later posing as Cambio .... *Pierre Cornay*
Hortensio, suitor to Bianca,
    later posing as Litio .... *Robert Mackintosh*
Petruchio, suitor to Kate .... *Antony Hoffman*
A Pedant, later posing as Vincentio ... *Ian Stewart*
Tranio, servant to Lucentio,
    later posing as Lucentio .... *Donald Logan*
Biondello, page to Lucentio .... *Benjamin Drexler*
Grumio, servant to Petruchio .... *William Hine*
Curtis, servant to Petruchio .... *Michael Burpee*
A Tailor .... *Patrick L'Anglais*
A Haberdasher .... *Richard Bardolis*
Katherine (Kate), the Shrew .... *Sheila Davis*
Bianca .... *Sally Green*
A Widow .... *Silvia Pakalns*
Servants to Baptista, Petruchio, Lucentio: *Emily Holly, Ann*
    Peacock, Jennifer Sloan, Nancy Milford, Elizabeth Wright
    (Induction, or Prologue, has been omitted)

Scene: Padua, near Verona

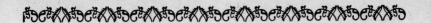

Edited, Produced and Directed by
NICHOLAS RUTHERFORD (B.A. OXON)
Formerly of St. Matthew's College, Kent, England

Incidental Music:
Composer: Antony Hoffman
Flautist: Janet Hale

Costumes:
Elizabeth Wright, Rachel Robinson, Emily Holly

Costume Assistants:
Bianca Kenner, Marie St. Jean, Mildred Hobbs, Jeanne Dupont, Sheila Davis, Sally Green, Janet Hale, Gabrielle Newman, Martha Duffield, Ellen Kopman, Jane Petrov, Angela Richardson, Silvia Pakalns, Claudia Thonnard, Marie Tavroges, Ann Peacock, Jennifer Sloan, Nancy Milford, Simone Gautier, William Kenner

Sets:
Designers: Pierre Cornay, Nicholas Rutherford
Builder: Gerald Dressler

Props:
Martha Duffield, Angela Richardson

Business Manager:
George Novotny

Director's Gal Friday:
Gabrielle Newman

We wish to express our gratitude to the parents of the cast, who financed the costume and set materials.

KENNER SCHOOL

RIVER ROAD • NEAR ST. HILAIRE • PROVINCE OF QUEBEC

Holly, Sally Green, and Janet Hale. Usually day boys were rather looked down on, but right now Matt was envied. However, when the four showed up at his house and were welcomed by his parents, he was as disappointed as the boarders had been by their very conventional, even outdated, femininity.

Still, they were girls, and the one called Sally was very pretty. He showed them up to the guest room, where two extra cots had been moved in. Curious, he lingered in the doorway as they began unpacking.

"I promised Kenny I'd bring only basic essentials for the weekend," the tall one called Mimi was saying. "So, besides clothes, I packed just my mice and my allergy pills."

She arranged a set of small cloth and china mice along the bureau. Toy mice! thought Matt scornfully. These kids must be emotionally retarded or something.

The pretty one called Sally seemed to be worrying about a fish. "I know Madame will feed him conscientiously, but I'm not sure she under*stands* fish."

Matt suddenly felt one of his outspoken moods coming over him.

"I must say, I'm disappointed in you kids. I thought you were all supposed to be so independent or something. And here you are, all dressed up like dolls, to impress Dr. Marston."

"To impress *him?*" It was the fat one called Janet, very indignant. "He's the *last* person we'd want to impress—his ideas on education are medi*eval!* Why, you're famous for being the strictest boarding school in the whole of Canada."

"North America," Matt corrected rather proudly. "We're fifty years old and three hundred years behind the times."

"Well, we'd never *dream* of dressing up to impress *you*. The Old-Fashioned Look just happens to be *in* right now. Last term it was the Dirty Look."

"The boys have been clean-cut for quite a while, though," added the dark-eyed one called Sheila. "They're getting pretty sick of it. Mike Fraser wants to start a Repulsive Look next year."

Matt was still unimpressed.

"I thought you were supposed to be so individualistic—not wearing the same clothes as each other all the time."

He couldn't suppress a grin of triumph at their faces; they were taken aback. They had no answer to that one. He'd seen through their silly, "individualistic" pretensions right away.

But suddenly the one called Janet smiled. It was a rather amused smile but good-natured.

"You know," she said, "you're kind of cute."

There were six productions in the festival, a matinee and an evening show each day: a very, very large dose of Shakespeare for one weekend. *Macbeth, Julius Caesar, As You Like It, The Taming of the Shrew,* and, by some mischance, two versions of *The Merchant of Venice,* one all girls.

The plays were held in the town auditorium. On Saturday afternoon the festival began, with Sedgewick's *Julius Caesar.* Mimi's prediction that their Shakespeare would be colorless and full of learned-by-rote reciting turned out to be very wrong. The production was lively and exciting; even Mr. Rutherford was impressed. He sought out the producer afterward to congratulate him.

The performance ended at five and was followed by a very large garden party, with nonalcoholic refreshments, on the Sedgewick lawns. Kenny commented enviously upon the beautiful condition of the grass. A loud roar arose from the conversations of nearly a thousand students.

There were boys in blazers with school crests, ties striped in school colors; girls in uniform tunics with a bright array of house ribbons and pins across their growing bosoms; girls and boys from the local high school in sports clothes and pretty dresses. But most striking were the Kenner students, especially the girls, who had all adopted the Old-Fashioned Look.

At first Jerry was a little on the defensive among these more conventional students, a little stiff. But he noticed that few of the other Kenner boys and girls seemed self-conscious. They chatted easily, impressing the other schools by their friendliness and self-assurance. Kenner students were seldom at a loss for a word.

Sheila was intoxicated by the presence of so many Sedgewick boys in their handsome dark-green blazers. A group gathered around her, asking curious questions about Kenner. She felt like a star being interviewed by the press and gave them a good performance.

"Of course we don't have to go to class if we feel emotionally unready," she remarked boastfully.

"Then don't you just fool around all the time?"

"Oh, no—we're very busy. For instance, Pierre Cornay is making a film. We saw the rushes last Saturday. His father's rather a big man in the National Film Board, and it does show his influence; but we feel Pierre is also evolving a style of his own."

"Is it true you kids have broken every single window in the school and the Kenners can't afford to repair them?"

"Why, heavens no," she said calmly. "If we ever *do* cause any damage, of course we pay for it ourselves. Anyway, why should we go around breaking windows? We don't want to *wreck* the school; we like being there."

"Seems like a pretty crazy place to me," one boy muttered skeptically. But he sounded rather envious.

Mimi and Janet were making the most of the Old-Fashioned Look—in very different ways. Janet joked about it and amused her audience, who thought her a scream. But Mimi couldn't resist playing it up. "Oh, I never play *sports* at Kenner," she insisted, "but I do like boating. Sometimes I take out a canoe and just drift for hours, admiring the beauties of nature."

Sally was surrounded by boys. "We bring our pets to school," she told them. "I brought my cat last term, but one of my roommates is allergic to them, so now I have just a fish."

"I wouldn't mind bringing my dog to school," said one boy, "but cats I can do without. They're so—so— Oh, I don't know . . ."

"Catlike?" Sally suggested, her bright blue eyes fixed on his.

"Well, yes!" Everybody chuckled. "Dogs are much more *human*," he added.

"I know," Sally agreed solemnly. "That's why they're so boring."

Then she grinned impishly and everybody laughed. Sally's giggle was deliciously infectious. Her long straight hair was pulled back in a pony tail, revealing a high forehead which gave her the look of an angelic child; but her eyes were full of mischief. They all adored her.

Jerry wandered from group to group, comparing different schools. Little as he approved of Kenner in many ways, he was glad he wasn't at Sedgewick; he considered it an expensive, snobbish prison. Suddenly he saw Phil. He was standing by himself and looked ill at ease.

"Phil! I'm so glad you could come!"

"I guess I shouldn't be at this party," Phil said defensively. "I came to see *Julius Caesar* and then got kind of swept along in the crowd. . . . But it seems just kids from the schools participating were invited. I just wanted to say Hello to you before I leave."

"Oh, stick around, for heaven's sake—relax. I'm glad you could make it."

Phil stared down at his feet. "I told you I'm not at school right now. I probably won't be next year either. But maybe the year after."

"Well, so long as you have a tutor you won't get behind. I'm going to a different school next year."

"Are you?" Phil looked up, surprised. "Why?"

"I only meant to come to Kenner for a year, as an experiment. Dad says I can go to our local high school next fall. He wouldn't want me to go to a regular boarding school; he and Mom think being cooped up with a lot of boys at my age is unhealthy. No Sedgewick for me, thank goodness. But no Kenner either."

"You seemed to be getting on so well at Kenner." Phil looked puzzled and even a little disappointed. "Don't you like it?"

"Oh, it's okay, in its way. *You* didn't like it much, did you?"

"No, but looking back I don't hate it like other schools I went to before. Nobody tried to make me do anything at Kenner. I was free to be just Phil the Pill. But you were nice to me."

Jerry felt a little guilty. After all, he hadn't really tried to get to know Phil at Kenner. He was friendly because he was friendly with everybody, in a casual way; somehow that went with being the school conservative. But in truth he hadn't really wanted to be very friendly with Phil. So neurotic a friend would have been a burden and an embarrassment.

"Jerry!" It was Mr. Rutherford. "I'd like to take a look at the sets with you—there'll have to be some adjustments for this stage."

"I'd better go now," said Jerry; "our show's tomorrow night, at eight. I hope you're coming?"

"Oh, yes. If it's half as good as *Julius Caesar,* it ought to be pretty great."

"Well, it's different—not so exciting but funny. Be sure and come backstage and congratulate us—unless it's a dismal flop, of course."

Mimi appeared just as Jerry was walking away. "These kids are so square, it's unbelievable," she remarked. "Imagine, I was just talking to one who things Pop art is *popular* art!" Suddenly she saw Phil. *"Phil!* How *are* you?"

"Okay," he replied, slightly defensive again.

"Gee, it's great to see you, really—we've missed you a lot. Things were more lively when you were around. Then Mr. Rutherford came— Oh, so much has happened, you wouldn't believe it. . . ." She talked on and on. Phil, at first stiff and rather sullen, relaxed a little, even smiled, at her dramatic description of the strike and the reform.

The huge auditorium was almost full; a roar of voices penetrated backstage. Putting last touches to her makeup, Sheila was terrified. She had known she would be nervous, but she hadn't expected to be in such a state of panic, alternately hot and cold with fear.

At least she looked good in her high-waisted Renaissance gown, deep golden-yellow over an olive-green underskirt. Her hair was pinned up under an olive-green headdress, wound about with gold ribbon. Mimi had been right to choose this yellow. Sheila had feared it would make her look more sallow; she had agreed with Rachel that red would be better. Mimi had insisted, and Mimi was right; she had an eye for color. This deep yellow made her skin, by contrast, a warm pale gold.

The makeup brought out her cheekbones, her dark eyes were huge and shining—with fright, mostly, but also vanity. She really did look gorgeous. If only Daddy could be here! Mother and Stan had flown to Toronto to see her performance; they were sitting out front right now.

Another wave of panic hit her. She turned to look at Sally and felt considerably less gorgeous. For Sally, in a blue dress and gold underskirt, was really adorable.

Janet, adjusting Sally's headdress, thought they made a lovely contrast: Sheila so golden, dress and skin, with her dark eyes and hair; Sally so blue, dress and eyes, her skin all pink and white, her hair pale gold. Their high-waisted gowns made the most of Sheila's beginnings of a bosom and Sally's already developing one.

Mimi complained, "Gee, just as I finally start to grow a bosom, I have to play a *man!*" She, Liz, and the other girls-as-boys wore baggy brown tunics and tights. Liz's tunic was heavily padded, to make her fat rather than buxom.

Tony knocked on the door of the girls' dressing room and entered to get some more grease paint. His legs, in olive-green tights, were a bit on the bony side; but otherwise he looked divine. His doublet was also green, his cape and hat golden yellow, his boots brown. Beyond him, out in the hall, hovered Mike and Pierre. Mike was a comical figure: wispy gray beard, purple gown, and an enormous, absurd gold hat. Money bags clinked heavily around his waist. Pierre was romantically attractive in a blue doublet and pale green tights. His legs were more shapely than Tony's.

Another knock. It was a delivery boy with two huge baskets of flowers—yellow roses, white chrysanthemums.

"Miss Sheila Davis," he announced.

Sheila, thrilled, looked at the cards. The roses were from

Daddy, the crysanthemums from Mother and Stan. "Good luck, darling. We'll be out watching you." It was great that they had been able to come; but it also made her more nervous.

"Aren't they lovely!" Mimi gushed. "Oh, dear, I better leave the room before I start sneezing—all that pollen . . ."

The Taming of the Shrew was a great success. The audience laughed uproariously. Some found Tony's incidental music (played by Janet on her flute) a little offbeat, perhaps not truly Elizabethan in spirit. Otherwise, it was a delight from beginning to end. Phil, coming backstage to congratulate them, was still smiling. "Your set was great," he told Jerry.

"Thank Pierre and Mr. Ruthy—they designed it. I just built it. A purely mechanical job."

After the play the Kenner students were invited back to Sedgewick Academy for a late supper with the faculty; the Sedgewick boys had had to go to bed. Tomorrow, after the final performance, there would be a dance in the gymnasium until one o'clock, and the prize would be presented by a drama critic from Toronto.

Sheila, conscious of being the star of the show, was very happy. Now she was more than just Somebody; she was the School Actress.

Mother and Stan were with her; the Marstons had urged her to bring them along. They were both tremendously impressed by her, and tremendously surprised. Mother kept looking at her in wonder, as though she could hardly believe it was her own sullen, brooding daughter who had acted Kate.

"You were amazing, dear. The moment you came on stage the audience sat up. And you looked lovely."

"Sorry it's all over?" Stan asked gently.

Sheila was grateful for his rare moment of understanding.

"Yes—awfully. We worked so hard, and made the costumes, and everything—and it's all gone in a couple of hours! But it was worth it."

She glanced at the next table, where Jerry was sitting. He was talking animatedly to Sally. Suddenly a sharp thrill of jealousy shot through her. Now that she came to think of it, she had seen Jerry talking animatedly to Sally rather often lately. And hadn't he taken her canoeing the other day? Sheila had been so concentrated on making sure he wasn't interested in Mimi, she foolishly hadn't noticed what was going on right before her eyes. Now, suddenly, she was certain. Some instinct told her that Sally was very much Jerry's type of girl—never Mimi, never Sheila. How *could* she have been so stupid? Sitting there, they looked so horribly right for each other somehow. An infuriatingly attractive couple.

Mother's face creased in her anxious little frown. "What's the matter, dear?"

"Oh—nothing."

"I guess you're getting on all right at Kenner now," Stan said uncertainly. "We were thinking of sending you to a day school next year, so we could see more of you. How do you feel?"

"Oh, Stan, I want to go back to Kenner," Sheila said urgently. *"Please!"*

Mother was smiling now. "Dear, I got your midterm report earlier this month, and it was very good, even better than the Easter one. All your teachers say how much you've blossomed out since Christmas. The Kenners feel you've developed more quickly than any student they've ever had. Of course you can go back!"

"Great! But, oh, Mother, *please* make Daddy agree!"

"I don't see how he can disagree when he's seen the report;

I'll send it to him. I only wish he could have seen you on stage!"

Mimi sat beside her in the bus on the way back to Matt's house, through the dark, quiet streets of this early-retiring Ontario town. Sally was a few seats behind, with Jerry. Mimi was very cheerful.

"I just can't wait for the dance tomorrow! I've decided to give up the Old-Fashioned Look and be sexy in my red silk. Sheila, I measured myself again this morning—and I haven't grown at all since March! I'm really beginning to dare hope this is *it* for me, heightwise. And Jerry *has* grown a bit, I think. So if I wear my flattest flats at the dance, we might just make it."

Sheila felt a sudden rush of irritation she couldn't contain.

"*I'll* tell you who he'll be dancing with tomorrow, you fool— our pretty little roommate."

"*Sally?* You *mean—?* Come *off* it, Sheil; you're just jealous."

Sheila didn't bother to deny it this time; she hardly cared if Mimi knew. But she was determined to dash any last hopes Mimi might have for herself.

"Well, take a look behind you. There they are, practically *necking,* for heaven's sake! How blind can you be?"

Actually they were just sitting together, talking quietly. But Mimi, having looked around, grew thoughtful. Gradually her mouth began to droop.

"Well . . . maybe you're right; maybe not. Oh, darn, it's so un*fair!* Sally doesn't *need* him; she can get any number of boys. Why does it have to be *him?*"

"How do you know she doesn't need him?" Sheila snapped irritably. "Maybe she needs all the boyfriends she can get to boost her ego. Maybe she's neurotic."

"No," said Mimi gloomily, "no such luck. I wish she *was—*

199

then I wouldn't be so jealous; I could comfort myself by telling myself Sally is neurotic. But she's not. She's just special."

Sheila said nothing, but she couldn't agree. She liked Sally these days (though not too much at the moment), but she still couldn't see anything so special about her. She just happened to be pretty, that was all.

Chapter Thirteen

*T*he big gymnasium was filled with boys and girls dancing to a small orchestra. The last play was over. There had been only one flop: an embarrassingly amateurish *As You Like It,* which the Toronto critic had walked out on. *Macbeth* and both productions of *The Merchant of Venice* were good— even the all-girls one, scheduled first, to give it a fair chance of an audience.

The dance had been going for about an hour. The actors, while enjoying it, were in suspense: the award was yet to be given. The prize was visible on the long table: a complete set of annotated Shakespeare, to go to the winning school.

Sheila was dancing with Matt, rather glumly. Over her shoulder she kept a sharp eye on Jerry and Sally, who had been together all evening. Mimi had reported seeing them exchange a kiss under the trees, on their way from the auditorium to the gym. A kind of rueful partnership had sprung up between Mimi and Sheila since last night, though Sheila rather resented the indignity of it. They took a gloomy satisfaction in observing all of Sally's and Jerry's movements and informing each other.

"Say," Matt exclaimed, making a slight face as the band launched into a Viennese waltz, "I hear there's a hootenanny outside. Want to go?"

Jerry and Sally had started to waltz, very fast—beautifully, of course. Suddenly Sheila was sick of them. "Yes," she said grate-fully. They pushed their way through the crowd and out into the night.

Mike, fearing a Sedgewick dance might be strictly square, had brought his banjo. His cousin had a guitar; Janet had her flute; a girl from the all-girls' *Merchant of Venice* unexpectedly produced an autoharp. They took so long getting tuned to-gether they almost lost their audience; but now, as Sheila and Matt emerged outdoors, they launched into song:

> Love, O love, O careless love,
> Love, O love, O careless love . . .

It was a very beautiful night, warm and soft under the trees. Sheila, wishing she had brought her guitar from Kenner, sang with the others, pouring all her mixed joys and heartaches into her voice. The instruments and the lusty voices of the singers drowned out the faint music from the big building ahead; and it seemed to dim Sally and Jerry a little, waltzing so smoothly inside. They all sat on the grass and sang more songs; Sheila was glad she had come. Matt put his arm around Sheila's shoulder. He was nice, but he wasn't Jerry. There was a new moon in the sky; the leaves rustled gently overhead; and Sheila sang. In spite of Jerry, life was full of endless possibilities: love—success—adventure. . . . She wasn't happy, but by now she was almost enjoying her gloom. It was all part of Life.

Word about the hootenanny must have spread indoors. In a short time the group under the trees grew larger, and voices swelled in a loud harmony. Phil was there, a little stiff but not hostile, with Mimi. Mimi, finally giving up on Jerry for once and for all, had decided against her red silk. She was being wistful and demure in her mauve. Phil sat beside her, rather good-looking in a light-blue suit. At his other side Janet played her flute, palely pretty and picturesque in the moonlight. It was all very romantic.

Mike sang his whole repertoire of original songs, which impressed the Sedgewick boys greatly. Jerry and Sally never appeared; they were too happy dancing.

Suddenly Mr. Rutherford called through the darkness. "Come on, all of you. It's time for the award!"

Everybody rose and hurried excitedly indoors. The Toronto critic and Dr. Marston sat at the table, Kenny and Willy nearby. Willy fidgeted as though he were in suspense; Kenny just smiled.

The critic rose and everyone was silent. He said all the productions had been impressive (ignoring the one flop) and his decision difficult. There were talented actors in every play, a good understanding of Shakespeare's meaning, good sets and costumes. But the winning play, he felt, was especially well paced, with a fine combination of freshness and professional polish. "And so it gives me great pleasure to announce the winner: *The Taming of the Shrew.*"

There was a great roar of clapping, and Mr. Rutherford went forward, almost shyly, to shake the critic's hand. Ben started a cheer for Mr. Rutherford, and others joined.

When the applause had died, Dr. Marston rose. He was a red-faced, stocky man with a reputation as a stern disciplinarian. He was smiling now.

"I'd like to add a few words, if I may. We were delighted to have the Kenner School come to our festival, and at such great distance; but I must add that, from what we'd heard of you all, we weren't quite sure what to expect!" (Laughter.) "Let me say now that, different though your system is from ours, and little as I approve of it on principle, I have been very favorably impressed by the Kenner boys and girls I have met this week-

end—and not only by your excellent performance. It's a pleasure indeed to meet boys of such unmistakable good breeding;
and your charmingly feminine girls are a delight. A rumor has
reached my ears that financial difficulties might cause the school
to be closed down. I sincerely hope that this is not so. Good
luck, Kenner School, and long life!"

There was another round of applause. Mr. Rutherford
looked at his English students and grinned broadly.

"Well," Sheila sighed as the group headed for the bus, much
later, "I guess I've had enough Shakespeare to last me a long,
long time."

Jerry appeared before her suddenly; Sally was ahead, talking
to Mr. Rutherford. "Sheila," he said, "I guess we owe a great
deal of our success to your talent."

"Come off it—you know all that 'professional polish' came
from Ruthy's relentless directing." Sheila wasn't going to put
up with any of his flattering charm—not now that she knew
about him and Sally.

"Well, you did contribute *something*. Gee, you certainly have
blossomed out this year. When I remember what a toad you
were last autumn—"

"What d'you mean, a toad?" she said indignantly.

"I mean—a toad, of course." His smile was teasing. "A dark,
sullen toad, sitting in a mud puddle without moving. But the
school's certainly done a lot for you."

"I suppose it's done nothing for you? I suppose you're so
perfect already, it couldn't do anything?"

"Well, I've tried my best to make sure it hasn't done *too*
much." He smiled, that irresistible twinkly, intimate smile, and
she smiled back in spite of herself. "Anyway, it has been fun,
but one year is enough."

"You're not coming back next year?"

"No, I never planned to. I'm going to the local high school at home. It's really more my kind of school."

"But won't you be a bit sad to leave?"

"Well, this last term's been a lot of fun. Sometimes I'm almost tempted to come back for one more year—"

"Oh, please, Jerry!" Suddenly she was very distressed by his leaving. "What will we do without our school conservative?"

He grinned. "Find another, of course."

Sheila entered the guest room at Matt's thoughtfully. Mimi and Janet were already undressing. "I guess Sally must be kissing Jerry good night," Janet was saying. "Poor Mimi, you must be consumed with jealousy. Your own roommate! Your best friend! Every girl's nightmare!"

"Oh, I've had crushes before—I'll get over it," said Mimi resignedly. "It's Sheila you should sympathize with—Hi, Sheila. . . . When you're first in love, you can't imagine ever getting over it. But then you do, and suddenly the guy's such a creep you think you must have been out of your mind."

"Sheila too?" said Janet. "Gee, this Jerry must have something. Glad _I_ didn't fall for him. He seems to be one of those charmers my big sister warned me about."

"Oh, shut up," said Sheila crossly. But then she added, "Jerry's not coming back next year." She told them what he had said. They were surprised and disapproving.

"We're losing so many boys," said Janet gloomily, "and we can't afford to lose _any_."

Sally came in, very pink and pretty.

"Hi, girls. Let's get to bed quickly; we have to drive all day tomorrow. I hope Gaby isn't carsick this time."

Mimi scowled at her. "All right, Sal: don't bother being embarrassed, or tactful, or avoiding me, or anything . . . I know _all_."

Sally didn't look the least embarrassed. "All?"

"You and Jerry."

"Oh. I thought you'd kind of gotten over him by now, Mimi."

"Well, let's say I'm resigned." She added, in catty triumph, "All right, have your little fling while you may; it can't last long. He won't be back next year."

"Oh, I know all about that, of course." Sally didn't seem at all sad. "He's going to write me and everything. And give me his class pin when he gets it." She began to brush her hair, smiling a secretive smile.

She's completely egocentric, Sheila thought. She doesn't care about Jerry at all, only wearing his class pin. At the same time, she wasn't quite positive. Mimi was always saying Sally was special. Maybe she loved in a special way too? One thing Sheila *was* sure of: she would never understand Sally.

"But *why* aren't you coming back?" Pierre persisted as he and Jerry undressed in the room they were sharing. "This term you really seemed to be *with* it."

Jerry tightened his lips irritably; he was getting sick and tired of all these questions. Why did he have to explain his decision, anyway? The reasons for his choice were so obvious. How *stupid* people were!

"I never *meant* to stay more than a year," he snapped. "My parents didn't expect me to. So drop it, will you?"

"Very well." Pierre's voice, as he sat on the edge of the bed pulling off his socks, was cool. His narrow green eyes looked at Jerry shrewdly. Jerry turned away.

At least Sally hadn't interrogated him. Sally had understood. "Oh, Jerry, I'll miss you!" was all she said when he told her. "You'll write me, won't you?"

"Every week," he promised, "and I'll send you my class pin."

Then they had kissed, under the trees, and afterward danced wildly, flushed and gay.

"Won't you miss Sally?" Pierre said teasingly.

"Oh, well . . ." Jerry shrugged his shoulders, elaborately casual. Sally was so pretty and gay, so full of life and so self-assured. She seemed perfectly happy just being her own graceful self—sometimes absorbed in private thoughts, sometimes full of laughter. "How long are you going to stay at Kenner?" he had asked her. "Oh, at least three more years," she said. "I love the school." Her words implied no criticism of him for wanting to leave; Sally didn't expect other people to be like her. But just for a moment he had felt a bit forlorn, like an outsider who would never be admitted into an exclusive club.

What a silly idea! He could stay on at Kenner if he wanted to. But he didn't want to end up like Tony, who was almost seventeen and still unsure about his future. Ex-Kennerites were sometimes ahead in their favorite subjects and behind in others. The school taught all subjects required for matriculation, if students chose to take them; but parents, however keen on progressive education when they first sent their children to Kenner, tended to become suddenly cautious when the students were about sixteen. They often sent them to a cram school to make sure they got into college. Tony, however, wasn't sure he wanted to go to college. He might go to music school, or travel and then decide. Seventeen years old, smart, talented, but still so uncertain!

Jerry was going on fifteen now; it was high time to leave. Next year he'd be a regular high school sophomore—not a "Kennerite."

"Well," Pierre said suddenly, "it's been fun with you at Kenner, *mon ami*. We've never had a school conservative before."

Jerry turned to see Pierre smiling. It was a teasing smile but warm. Jerry smiled back.

"I've never *been* a school conservative before. In fact, I used to be considered rather liberal!" And they both laughed.

Mike had long since given up playing his banjo: nobody wanted to sing anymore; they were too tired. The return journey was tedious without the festival to look forward to. At least Gaby wasn't sick. She slept nearly all the time; Mildred had given her a powerful pill.

Sheila and Mimi, still joined in their half-hearted partnership, sat together. Mimi was fairly cheerful.

"I promised to write Phil and tell him about school—and he'll write me about his analysis. I'm not sure if I can get really interested in him or not. He's still so neurotic, but at least he's not a creep, and he's tall. So maybe."

Ben exclaimed suddenly, "Gee, now those poor guys at Sedgewick are all frantically cramming for exams. Lucky us! Just two weeks of swimming and boating and marine biology, and then the holidays."

Mr. Rutherford looked around.

"Now, what makes you so sure you won't have exams? Seven of you certainly will, for I intend to give a three-hour English exam next Monday. So start cramming."

There were moans of dismay from his students.

"Oh, Mr. *Ruthy*—"

"Aw, gee, Nick—"

"We *never* have exams—"

"Rosalie never—"

"Now, let me tell you something about Rosalie," Kenny broke in. She was sitting beside Mr. Rutherford. "I wasn't going to tell you, but I might as well. Rosalie's leaving was no accident; it wasn't because of illness—she's as healthy as a horse. We usually like to leave teachers as free as possible, but we couldn't help disapproving of some of the things she was doing with you all. Not her academic methods but the way she tried to psychoanalyze you so glibly. Rosalie is keen and intelligent but awfully glib; she thinks she knows everything, but most of it she's learned from books, and Willy and I found her analyses very shallow. Also we felt she was going too far; it wasn't her business. So anyway, just before the Christmas holidays I discussed the matter with her. She got very indignant and proud, and resigned on the spot."

"So *that* explains it!" Janet exclaimed. "I always *thought* there was something funny about her leaving."

"Yes. So then Willy and I asked Nicholas if he'd step in for the rest of the year, and he graciously agreed. We decided he might be an interesting change."

"Oh! I thought you just got him 'cause you were desperate—"

"Come on, now, Janet"—Kenny grinned at her—"we wouldn't get just *anyone!* No, it's true he was a last-minute substitute, and we'd have looked for somebody else if we'd had time; but we also thought Nicholas might be interestingly different. Of course Rosalie was a perfectly good teacher so long as she didn't get too personal—"

"We all liked our Rosie, except when she was nosy," Sally put in.

"Exactly! But Willy and I felt you were growing a bit rigid in your ideas of how you should be taught and a change might be invigorating."

Mr. Rutherford's eyes twinkled merrily. "Don't worry," he said, "you won't have to put up with me next year. You'll have another new teacher. I'm retiring from teaching for good."

"Oh, *Nicholas,*" Liz exclaimed, "I was planning to take your course next year! It'll be my last year at Kenner."

"I'm sorry," he said gently. "You see, Liz, when I retired

from teaching to write, I really meant it. I agreed to help out the Kenners because Kenny is an old friend; but now I must go back to my writing."

Jerry, seated beside Sally across the aisle, smiled at Mr. Rutherford approvingly. It made him feel better, somehow, to find that somebody else was leaving, especially since it was good old Ruthy.

"We'll miss you, Mr. Ruthy," Sheila said sadly. At the same time she had a half-guilty feeling that maybe it was just as well. Mr. Rutherford would never be very popular as a teacher. With the festival and his current prestige as director in the background, his class might dwindle to almost nothing, for so many other courses were available. Next year they would have a new teacher, they would act their own plays again, and Mr. Rutherford would do his writing. Maybe this way was best for everyone. "Won't you miss us too?" she asked hopefully.

"Well,"—his eyes were teasing—"perhaps just a little." Everybody smiled, but they were sad. In spite of everything, they had all grown very fond of Nicholas Rutherford.

Willy cheered them with an announcement.

"Anyway, the school will keep going," he said, turning a little away from the wheel to address the crowded bus. "Tony's father and Sheila's stepfather have both given us generous donations; and I think we might be getting something from the Bartells after all. So at least we can pay off our debts."

Everybody cheered, including Mr. Rutherford.

They entered the village, and everyone fell silent again. Sheila eyed Jerry and Sally rather sulkily. His dark head and her blond one were very close together.

But suddenly she laughed. "What a year, Mimi . . . three roommates all in love with the same guy. What a comedy!"

"A *black* comedy," said Mimi grimly. She relapsed into a

frowning silence. Then her face cleared. "You know, I've decided that in spite of everything, this has been a valuable year for me. Last year was more fun, but this year has been more of an *experience*. Because I've *suffered*. You can't be mature until you've really *suffered*."

"It's been quite a year for me, too," said Sheila.

"Well, yes, but you haven't *suffered* much, have you?—except for Jerry. Otherwise, it's been a very successful year for you. Never mind," she added kindly, "maybe next year will be your suffering year."

"Gee, I hope *not*." Sheila opened her eyes wide in mock horror, then smiled at Mimi tolerantly. Mimi *meant* well—or did she really? Oh, Mimi was okay. But there was a lot she didn't understand. Hard to remember that only a few months ago Mimi had seemed so sophisticated.

They passed through the village. The evening sun glinted on the river; they were almost home. Cows and horses grazed in the St. Jean's fields. The orchard was in bloom. Soon another apple season would begin—just as the supply in the school basement was running low.

The bus turned in at the driveway and they saw the familiar overgrown lawn, the familiar dirty red-brick house. It looked dirtier somehow.

"Oh, dear," said Kenny. "We really must get to work on the grass."

Madame appeared in the doorway, waving a welcome with a dishtowel.

"Hello, Madame!" Willy called. "What's for dinner?"

And Sheila replied quickly, "Apples, of course!"

HARPER TROPHY BOOKS
you will enjoy reading

The Little House Books by *Laura Ingalls Wilder*

J1	Little House in the Big Woods
J2	Little House on the Prairie
J3	Farmer Boy
J4	On the Banks of Plum Creek
J5	By the Shores of Silver Lake
J6	The Long Winter
J7	Little Town on the Prairie
J8	These Happy Golden Years
J31	The First Four Years

J9	Journey from Peppermint Street *by Meindert DeJong*
J10	Look Through My Window *by Jean Little*
J11	The Noonday Friends *by Mary Stolz*
J12	White Witch of Kynance *by Mary Calhoun*
J14	Catch As Catch Can *by Josephine Poole*
J15	Crimson Moccasins *by Wayne Dyre Doughty*
J16	Gone and Back *by Nathaniel Benchley*
J17	The Half Sisters *by Natalie Savage Carlson*
J18	A Horse Called Mystery *by Marjorie Reynolds*
J19	The Seventeenth-Street Gang *by Emily Cheney Neville*
J20	Sounder *by William H. Armstrong*

J21	The Wheel on the School *by Meindert DeJong*
J22	The Secret Language *by Ursula Nordstrom*
J23	A Kingdom in a Horse *by Maia Wojciechowska*
J24	The Golden Name Day *by Jennie D. Lindquist*
J25	Hurry Home, Candy *by Meindert DeJong*
J26	Walk the World's Rim *by Betty Baker*
J27	Her Majesty, Grace Jones *by Jane Langton*
J28	Katie John *by Mary Calhoun*
J29	Depend on Katie John *by Mary Calhoun*
J30	Honestly, Katie John! *by Mary Calhoun*

HARPER & ROW, PUBLISHERS, INC.
10 East 53rd Street, New York, New York 10022